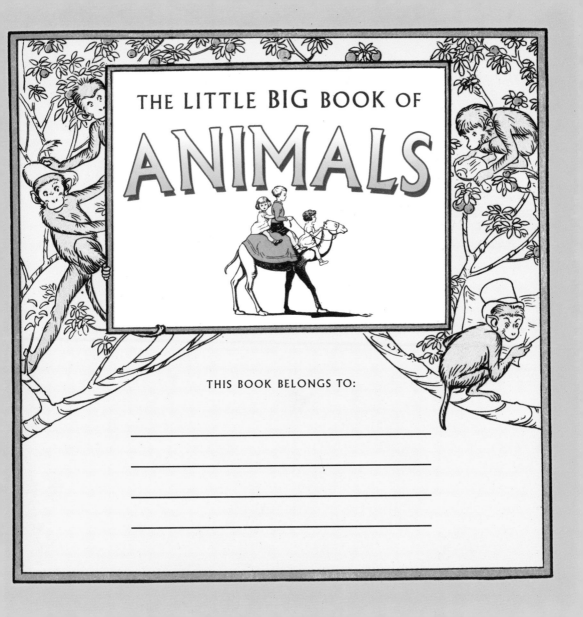

# THE LITTLE BIG BOOK OF
# ANIMALS

THIS BOOK BELONGS TO:

welcome
BOOKS

New York • San Francisco

Edited by **Lena Tabori**
& **Katrina Fried**

*Designed by* **Jon Glick**

The Little Big Book of

# ANIMALS

# CONTENTS

## ACTIVITIES

## SAYINGS, WORD GAMES, JOKES & RIDDLES

## RECIPES

Published in 2002 by Welcome Books,
An imprint of Welcome Enterprises, Inc.
6 West 18th Street, 3rd Floor, New York, NY, 10011
(212) 989-3200; Fax (212) 989-3205
email: info@welcomebooks.biz
www.welcomebooks.biz

Designer: Jon Glick
Project Directors: Katrina Fried and Natasha Tabori Fried
Editorial & Research Assistants: Lawrence Chesler,
Rachel Hertz, Nicholas Liu, Jacinta O'Halloran

Select stories retold by Sara Baysinger and Matthew Webber
Music arrangement by Frank Zuback
Activities by Nicholas Liu and Katrina Fried
Sayings by Rachel Hertz
Recipes by Lena Tabori

Distributed to the trade in the U.S. and Canada by
Andrews McMeel Distribution Services
Order Department and Customer Service: (800) 223-2336
Orders Only Fax: (800) 943-9831

Library of Congress Control Number: 2001056800

ISBN 0-941807-56-8

Printed in Singapore
First Edition
10 9 8 7 6 5 4 3 2

# FOREWORD

*By Katrina Fried*

At the age of eight, my favorite film was *Pete's Dragon*, my favorite TV show was *Lassie*, and my all-time favorite book was *Charlotte's Web*. If there was an animal in it, I wanted to read it or watch it. I adored Disney's world of animated creatures, and spent hours immersed in such classic fiction as *The Velveteen Rabbit* and Rudyard Kipling's *Just So* stories. I was endlessly in love with the idea that animals were like people, able to communicate, to love, to dream, to experience joy and even sadness.

We were an extremely pet-friendly family, and welcomed three dogs, three cats, a mouse, a gerbil, a half dozen birds, and an untold number of fish into our home throughout my childhood years. One of our cats, two of our dogs, and five of our fish had litters (which led to our second cat, our third dog, and *many* more fish.) Nearly all our animals were named after favorite literary and TV characters: Benson—the parakeet; Hot Lips—the finch (named after Loretta Swit's character on *M.A.S.H.*); Solo—the mutt (named after the title character in a book about Australian wild dogs); Boo—Solo's puppy (named after Boo Radley in *To Kill A Mockingbird*); Mickey—the black cat (named after the most famous of mice); and Tigger—the striped guppy, to name just a few!

All these animals, both real and fictional, peopled my young imagination. They helped shape my hobbies, tastes, and perceptions of the world. My introduction to the classic equestrian novels *Black Beauty*, *The Black Stallion*, and *National Velvet* resulted in a love for horses and inspired me to learn how to ride. To this day, I have no taste for truffles because Babar's father was killed by a poisonous mushroom, and I still dream of sharing a plate of spaghetti with my true love that ends in a kiss as it did in *Lady and the Tramp*. From my own pets, I learned about friendship, acceptance, and loss. In their adorable way, our dogs and cats, in particular, showed me the ultimate standard for unconditional love and loyalty. Even their passings taught me important lessons about the value of life and the reality of death.

*The Little Big Book of Animals* celebrates our childhood love for all creatures great and small and the lessons they teach us. It contains many of the best stories, poems, activities, games, sayings, and songs about our animal friends. Together my mother and I researched and assembled the contents of this anthology. Each piece was chosen with care to bring you and your children moments of genuine joy, tenderness, excitement, curiosity, surprise, peace, and perhaps nostalgia. Most important, we hope it will inspire a life-long love of animals. There can be no greater gift.

# THE TALE OF PETER RABBIT

*BY BEATRIX POTTER*

Once upon a time there were four little Rabbits, and their names were—Flopsy, Mopsy, Cotton-tail, and Peter.

They lived with their mother in a sand bank, underneath the root of a very big-fir tree.

"Now, my dears," said old Mrs. Rabbit one morning, "you may go into the fields or down the lane, but don't go into Mr. McGregor's garden; your Father had an accident there; he was put in a pie by Mrs. McGregor.

"Now run along, and don't get into mischief. I am going out."

Then old Mrs. Rabbit took a basket and her umbrella and went through the wood to the baker's.

She bought a loaf of brown bread and five currant buns.

Flopsy, Mopsy, and Cotton-tail, who were good little bunnies, went down the lane to gather black-berries; but Peter, who was very naughty, ran straight away to Mr. McGregor's garden, and squeezed under the gate!

11

First he ate some lettuces and some French beans; and then he ate some radishes; and then, feeling rather sick, he went to look for some parsley.

But round the end of a cucumber frame, whom should be meet but—

Mr. McGregor!

Mr. McGregor was on his hands and knees planting out young cabbages, but he jumped up and ran after Peter, waving a rake and calling out, "Stop thief!"

Peter was most dreadfully frightened; he rushed all over the garden, for he had forgotten the way back to the gate.

He lost one of his shoes among the cabbages, and the other shoe amongst the potatoes.

After losing them, he ran on four legs and went faster, so that I think he might have got away altogether if he had not unfortunately run into a gooseberry net, and got caught by the large buttons on his jacket. It was a blue jacket with brass buttons, quite new.

Peter gave himself up for lost, and shed big tears; but his sobs were overheard by some friendly sparrows, who flew to him in great excitement, and implored him to exert himself.

Mr. McGregor came up with a sieve, which he intended to pop upon the top of Peter; but Peter wriggled out just in time, leaving his jacket behind him.

And rushed into the tool shed, and jumped into a can. It would have been a beautiful thing to hide in, if it had not had so much water in it.

Mr. McGregor was quite sure that Peter was somewhere in the tool-shed, perhaps hidden underneath a flowerpot. He began to turn them over carefully, looking under each.

Presently Peter sneezed—
"Kertyschoo!" Mr. McGregor was after
him in no time and tried to put his
foot upon Peter, who jumped out of a
window upsetting three plants.
The window was too small for Mr.
McGregor, and he was tired of running
after Peter. He went back to his work.

Peter sat down to rest; he was out
of breath and trembling with fright,
and he had not the least idea which
way to go. Also he was very damp with
sitting in that can.

After a time he began to wander
about, going lippity-lippity—not very
fast, and looking all around.

He found a door in a wall; but it
was locked, and there was no room for a
fat little rabbit to squeeze underneath.

An old mouse was running in and
out over the stone doorstep, carrying

peas and beans to her family in the
wood. Peter asked her the way to the
gate, but she had such a large pea in
her mouth that she could not answer.
She only shook her head at him. Peter
began to cry.

Then he tried to find his way
straight across the garden, but he
became more and more puzzled.
Presently, he came to a pond where Mr.
McGregor filled his water-cans.

A white cat was staring at some
goldfish; she sat very, very still, but
now and then the tip of her tail
twitched as if it were alive. Peter
thought it best to go away without
speaking to her; he had heard about
cats from his cousin, little Benjamin
Bunny.

He went back towards the tool-
shed, but suddenly, quite close to him,

he heard the noise of a hoe—sc-r-ritch, scratch, scratch, scritch.

Peter scuttered underneath the bushes.

But presently, as nothing happened, he came out, and climbed upon a wheelbarrow, and peeped over. The first thing he saw was Mr. McGregor hoeing onions. His back was turned towards Peter, and beyond him was the gate!

Peter got down very quietly off the wheel-barrow, and started running as fast as he could go, along a straight walk behind some black-currant bushes.

Mr. McGregor caught sight of him at the corner, but Peter did not care. He slipped underneath the gate, and was safe at last in the wood outside the garden.

Mr. McGregor hung up the little jacket and the shoes for a scare-crow to frighten the blackbirds.

Peter never stopped running or looked behind him till he got home to the big fir-tree.

He was so tired that he flopped down upon the nice soft sand on the floor of the rabbit-hole, and shut his eyes. His mother was busy cooking; she wondered what he had done with his clothes. It was the second little jacket and pair of shoes that Peter had lost in a fortnight!

I am sorry to say that Peter was not very well during the evening. His mother put him to bed, and made some camomile tea; and she gave a dose of it to Peter! "One tablespoonful to be taken at bedtime."

But Flopsy, Mopsy, and Cottontail had bread and milk and blackberries for supper.

15

# BUNNY FRUIT SALAD

**S**erve fruit salad in the shape of a bunny rabbit and turn a healthy snack into a fun treat that will hop right off the plate into little mouths.

*4 leaves iceberg lettuce, washed*

*1 ripe pear,
peeled and sliced in half*

*4 dried cranberries*

*2 raspberries*

*2 tablespoons cottage cheese*

*4 blanched almonds*

1. Place 2 leaves of lettuce on each plate to make a grassy lawn.

2. To make each bunny's body, place half a pear, flat side down, on top of the lettuce leaves.

3. Lightly press two dried cranberries into each pear to make the eyes, a raspberry to make the nose, two almonds to make the ears, and a scoop of cottage cheese to make the cottontail. Serve immediately.

*Serves two*

# OLD MACDONALD

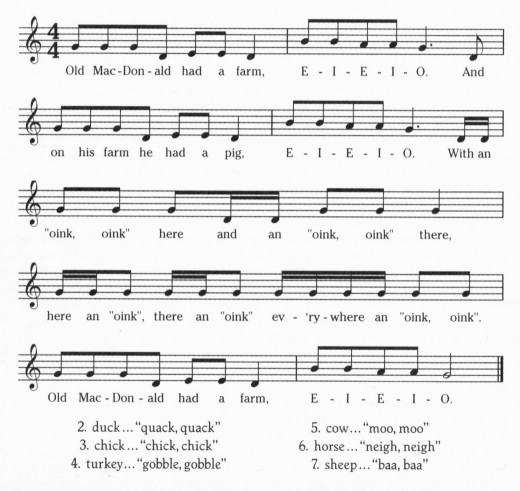

# Animal Tracks

Here's a farmyard in the snow,
Footprints going to and fro.
Daddy to the stable went,
To the henhouse Ted was sent,
All the fowls came running out,
Betty scattered corn about.
Turkeys, ducks, and pigeons fleet
Came to gobble up the treat.
From the sty the fat old sow,
From the stall the gentle cow
Came to see what could be found.
Puss was chased by Pat, the hound.
Dobbin came up for a drink.
Can you trace them, do you think?

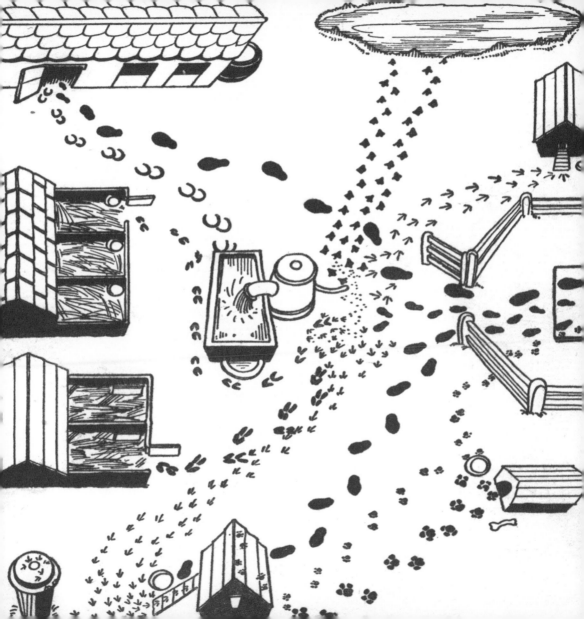

# FARM ANIMAL FACTS

* A female goat is called a nanny, a male goat is called a billy, and baby goats are called kids!

* In just one day, a dairy cow can make up to 125 pounds of saliva!

* There are more chickens than

* What do you call the breed of chicken that closely resembles a turkey? A "Turken" of course!

* A foal (baby horse) is born with nearly fully grown legs and can walk within 1–2 hours.

24

✳ The smallest horse on record was an American
Falabella called Little Pumpkin, who was only 14 inches high!

✳ The French and Italians use pigs to sniff out
hard-to-find mushrooms called truffles.

there are people in the world.

✳ If you plan on visiting Gainesville, Georgia—known as the chicken
capitol of the world—make sure you wash your hands before sitting down
to dinner. In Gainesville, it's against the law to eat chicken with a fork!

✳ Next time Mom says no to getting a puppy,
try asking for a pig! They make loving pets and
learn tricks more easily than dogs.

# THE ANSWERS
## BY ROBERT CLAIRMONT

"When did the world begin and how?"
I asked a lamb, a goat, a cow:

"What's it all about and why?"
I asked a hog as he went by:

"Where will the whole thing end, and when?"
I asked a duck, a goose, a hen:

And I copied all the answers too,
A quack, a honk, an oink, a moo.

# Animal Sayings
## And what they mean

### March comes in like a lion, and goes out like a lamb
*March begins roughly, when it's winter, and ends gently, when it's spring.*

### Take the bull by the horns
*Face your challenges head on.*

### The straw that broke the camel's back
*The thing that makes you finally say, "Enough is enough!"*

# When pigs fly
*Never!*

# Get someone's goat
*Really bug someone.*

# Two shakes of a lamb's tail
*Less time than it took to read this sentence!*

# Don't have a cow
*Relax!*

# Happy as a pig in mud
*Feeling great because you're doing something you really enjoy.*

# CHARLOTTE'S WEB

*BY E. B. WHITE*

*Charlotte's Web tells the story of a lovable pig named Wilbur and his colorful barnyard pals. In this excerpt, Wilbur seeks out the owner of the mysterious voice who called out to him in the dark the night before.*

The night seemed long. Wilbur's stomach was empty and his mind was full. And when your stomach is empty and your mind is full, it's always hard to sleep.

A dozen times during the night Wilbur woke and stared into the blackness, listening to the sounds and trying to figure out what time it was. A barn is never perfectly quiet. Even at midnight there is usually something stirring.

The first time he woke, he heard Templeton gnawing a hole in the grain bin. Templeton's teeth scraped loudly against the wood and made quite a racket. "That crazy rat!" thought Wilbur. "Why does he have to stay up all night, grinding his clashers and destroying people's property? Why can't he go to sleep, like any decent animal?"

The second time Wilbur woke, he heard the goose turning on her nest and chuckling to herself.

"What time is it?" whispered Wilbur to the goose.

"Probably-obably-obably about half-past eleven," said the goose. "Why aren't you asleep, Wilbur?"

"Too many things on my mind," said Wilbur.

"Well," said the goose, "that's not *my* trouble. I have nothing at all on my mind, but I've too many things under my behind. Have you ever tried to sleep while sitting on eight eggs?"

"No," replied Wilbur. "I suppose it *is* uncomfortable. How long does it take a goose egg to hatch?"

"Approximately-oximately thirty days, all told," answered the goose. "But I cheat a little. On warm afternoons, I just pull a little straw over the eggs and go out for a walk."

Wilbur yawned and went back to sleep. In his dreams he heard again the voice saying, "I'll be a friend to you. Go to sleep—you'll see me in the morning."

About half an hour before dawn, Wilbur woke and listened. The barn was still dark. The sheep lay motionless. Even the goose was quiet. Overhead, on the main floor, nothing stirred: the cows were resting, the horses dozed. Templeton had quit work and gone off somewhere on an errand. The only sound was a slight scraping noise from the rooftop, where the weather vane swung back and forth. Wilbur loved the barn when it was like this—calm and quiet, waiting for light.

"Day is almost here," he thought.

Through a small window, a faint gleam appeared. One by one the stars went out. Wilbur could see the goose a few feet away. She sat with head tucked under a wing. Then he could see the sheep and the lambs. The sky lightened.

"Oh, beautiful day, it is here at last! Today I shall find my friend."

Wilbur looked everywhere. He searched his pen thoroughly. He examined the window ledge, stared up at the ceiling. But he saw nothing new. Finally he decided he would have to speak up. He hated to break the lovely stillness of dawn by using his voice, but he couldn't think of any other way to locate the mysterious new friend who was nowhere to be seen. So Wilbur cleared his throat.

"Attention, please!" he said in a loud, firm voice. "Will the party who addressed me at bedtime last night kindly make himself or herself known by giving an appropriate sign or signal!"

Wilbur paused and listened. All the other animals lifted their heads and stared at him. Wilbur blushed. But he was determined to get in touch with his unknown friend.

"Attention, please!" he said. "I will repeat the message. Will the party who addressed me at bedtime last night kindly speak up. Please tell me where you are, if you are my friend!"

The sheep looked at each other in disgust.

"Stop your nonsense, Wilbur!" said the oldest sheep. "If you have a new friend here, you are probably disturbing his rest; and the quickest way to spoil a friendship is to wake somebody up in the morning before he is ready. How can you be sure your friend is an early riser?"

"I beg everyone's pardon," whispered Wilbur. "I didn't mean to be objectionable."

He lay down meekly in the manure, facing the door. He did not know it, but his friend was very near. And the old sheep was right—the friend was still asleep.

Soon Lurvy appeared with slops for breakfast. Wilbur rushed out, ate everything in a hurry, and licked the trough. The sheep moved off down the lane, the gander waddled along behind them, pulling grass. And then, just as Wilbur was settling down for his morning nap, he heard again the thin voice that had addressed him the night before.

"Salutations!" said the voice.

Wilbur jumped to his feet. "Salu-*what*?" he cried.

"Salutations!" repeated the voice.

"What are *they*, and where are *you*?" screamed Wilbur. "Please, *please*, tell me where you are. And what are salutations?"

"Salutations are greetings," said the voice. "When I say 'salutations,' it's just my fancy way of saying hello or good morning. Actually, it's a silly expression, and I am surprised that I used it at all. As for my whereabouts, that's easy. Look up here in the corner of the doorway! Here I am. Look, I'm waving!"

At last Wilbur saw the creature that had spoken to him in such a kindly way. Stretched across the upper part of the doorway was a big spider web, and hanging from the top of the web, head down, was a large grey spider. She was about the size of a gumdrop. She had eight legs, and she was waving one of them at Wilbur in friendly greeting. "See me now?" she asked.

"Oh, yes indeed," said Wilbur. "Yes indeed! How are you? Good morning! Salutations! Very pleased to meet you. What is your name, please? May I have your name?"

"My name," said the spider, "is Charlotte."

"Charlotte what?" asked Wilbur, eagerly.

"Charlotte A. Cavatica. But just call me Charlotte."

"I think you're beautiful," said Wilbur.

"Well, I *am* pretty," replied Charlotte. "There's no denying that. Almost all spiders are rather nice-looking. I'm not as flashy as some, but I'll do. I wish I could see you, Wilbur, as clearly as you can see me."

"Why can't you?" asked the pig. "I'm right here."

"Yes, but I'm nearsighted," replied Charlotte. "I've always been dreadfully nearsighted. It's good in some ways, not so good in others. Watch me wrap up this fly."

A fly that had been crawling along Wilbur's trough had flown up and blundered into the lower part of Charlotte's web and was tangled in the sticky threads. The fly was beating its wings furiously, trying to break loose and free itself.

"First," said Charlotte, "I dive at him." She plunged headfirst toward the fly. As she dropped, a tiny silken thread unwound from her rear end.

"Next, I wrap him up." She grabbed the fly, threw a few jets of silk around it, and rolled it over and over, wrapping it so that it couldn't move. Wilbur watched in horror. He could hardly believe what he was seeing, and although he detested flies, he was sorry for this one.

"There!" said Charlotte. "Now I knock him out, so he'll be more comfortable." She bit the fly. "He can't feel a thing now," she remarked. "He'll make a perfect breakfast for me."

"You mean you *eat* flies?" gasped Wilbur.

35

"Certainly. Flies, bugs, grass-hoppers, choice beetles, moths, butter-flies, tasty cockroaches, gnats, midges, daddy longlegs, centipedes, mosquitoes, crickets—anything that is careless enough to get caught in my web. I have to live, don't I?"

"Why, yes, of course," said Wilbur. "Do they taste good?"

"Delicious!" said Charlotte, and her pleasant, thin voice grew even thinner and more pleasant.

"Don't say that!" groaned Wilbur. "Please don't say things like that!"

"Why not? It's true, and I have to say what is true. I am not entirely happy about my diet of flies and bugs, but it's the way I'm made. A spider has to pick up a living somehow or other, and I happen to be a trapper. I just naturally build a web and trap flies and other insects. My mother was a trapper before me. Her mother was a trapper before her. All our family have been trappers. Way back for thousands and thousands of years we spiders have been laying for flies and bugs."

"It's a miserable inheritance," said Wilbur, gloomily.

"Yes, it is," agreed Charlotte. "But I can't help it. I don't know how the first spider in the early days of the world happened to think up this fancy idea of spinning a web, but she did, and it was clever of her, too. And since then, all of us spiders have had to work the same trick. It's not a bad pitch, on the whole."

"It's cruel," replied Wilbur, who did not intend to be argued out of his position.

"Well, *you* can't talk," said Charlotte. "*You* have your meals brought to you in a pail. Nobody feeds me. I have to get my own living. I live by my wits. I have to be sharp and clever, lest I go hungry. I have to think things out, catch what I can, take what comes. And it just so happens, my friend, that what comes is flies and insects and bugs. And *further*more," said Charlotte, shaking one of her legs, "do you realize that if I didn't catch bugs and eat them, bugs would increase and multiply and get so numerous that they'd destroy the earth, wipe out everything?"

"Really?" said Wilbur. "I wouldn't want that to happen. Perhaps your web is a good thing after all."

Charlotte stood quietly over the fly, preparing to eat it. Wilbur lay down and closed his eyes. He was tired from his wakeful night and from the excitement of meeting someone for the first time. A breeze brought him the smell of clover—the sweet-smelling world beyond his fence. "Well," he thought, "I've got a new friend, all right. But what a gamble friendship is! Charlotte is fierce, brutal, scheming, bloodthirsty— everything I don't like. How can I learn to like her, even though she is pretty and, of course, clever?"

Wilbur was merely suffering the doubts and fears that often go with finding a new friend. In good time he was to discover that he was mistaken about Charlotte. Underneath her rather bold and cruel exterior, she had a kind heart, and she was to prove loyal and true to the very end.

# THE ANIMAL FAIR

I went to the an-i-mal fair; the birds and the beasts were there. The big ba-boon by the light of the moon, was comb-ing his au-burn hair. The mon-key, he got drunk; he sat on the el-e-phant's trunk. The el-e-phant sneezed and fell to his knees and that was the end of the monk.

# KOKO'S KITTEN

### BY DR. FRANCINE PATTERSON

*This is the true story of an unusual friendship between a gorilla named Koko and a kitten named Ball. Koko is a very special gorilla who lives in captivity and has been taught to communicate through sign language. Three days before her twelfth birthday Koko asked her trainer, Dr. Francine Patterson, for a cat as a birthday present. In her book* Koko's Kitten, *Dr. Patterson recalls how Koko met her first feline friend, and the touching relationship that developed between them.*

Things don't always happen quickly where we live. Every day is full of its own activities. So it was almost six months later when Karen, one of my assistants, arrived with three kittens. The kittens had been abandoned by their mother and raised by a dog, a Cairn terrier.

Karen showed the kittens to Koko.

"Love that," Koko signed.

"Which one do you want?" we asked.

"That," signed Koko, pointing to the tailless tabby.

I am not sure why Koko picked the gray tabby as her favorite. I never asked her. Perhaps it was because he didn't have a tail—a gorilla has no tail.

# KOKO'S KITTEN

That night, all three kittens went home with Karen. Two days later, the kittens came back for another visit. Koko was happy to see them.

"Visit love tiger cat," Koko signed.

First she picked up the smoky gray and white one. Then Koko took the tailless tabby and carried him on her thigh. After a while, she pushed him up onto the back of her neck.

"Baby," Koko signed.

She cradled the tabby in her legs and examined its paws. Koko squeezed, and the tabby's claws came out.

"Cat do scratch," Koko signed. "Koko love."

"What will you name the kitty?" I asked.

"All Ball," Koko signed.

"Yes," I said. "Like a ball, he has no tail."

Ball stayed overnight as a visiting kitten. By the end of the week, Ball was a permanent member of our household.

Koko had her kitten at last.

For the first few weeks, Ball lived in my house. Every evening at six o'clock, I would take Ball to Koko's trailer for an evening visit. I carried the kitten in my pocket as I prepared Koko for bed. Koko soon grew accustomed to this routine.

"What happens at night?" I asked.

"All Ball," signed Koko.

"Right," I said. "Ball visits you at night."

When he was older, Ball snuck into Koko's trailer by himself. It worried me in the beginning. I did not know how Koko would treat the kitten unsupervised. As it turned out, Koko was always gentle. Ball was never afraid of her.

Kittens should not be separated from their mothers until they are at least six weeks old. Poor Ball was abandoned by his mother at birth, which might have accounted for some of his faults.

Ball was an unusual cat. He was very aggressive. He would go up to people and bite them for no reason. He would bite Koko, too.

"Cat bite. Obnoxious," Koko signed, but she never struck back.

Koko did not like to be scratched or bitten, but she loved Ball in spite of his naughty behavior.

"Tell me a story about Ball," I said.

"Koko love Ball," she signed.

Koko treated Ball as if he were her baby.

The very first time she picked him up, she tried to tuck him in her thigh. That's where mother gorillas put their infants. Older babies are carried on their mothers' backs. Koko tried this with Ball, too.

Koko was a good gorilla mother. She combed and petted Ball to keep him clean. She also examined his eyes, ears, and mouth to make sure he was healthy. It was Koko who discovered Ball's ear mites.

Ball was often a topic of conversation during Koko's lessons.

"Love visit," Koko signed when Ball and I arrived for a morning lesson.

"Ball," I said.

"Trouble," signed Koko. "Love."

Koko loves to play games. Her favorites are "chase," "blow-it," and "tickle."

Koko likes to be tickled, and she thinks that others will like it, too.

"Tickle," Koko signed to Ball when they were lying on the floor together.

Ball was not a good tickler, nor did he like to be tickled. So Koko and I pretended. I tickled Koko while carrying the kitten in my hand. Koko thought this was very funny.

Koko did not realize that kittens don't necessarily enjoy gorilla games. Koko did understand that kittens like warmth, affection, and attention. And Koko supplied plenty.

## Monkey business
*Goofing around—*
*in a naughty way!*

## Monkey see, monkey do
*You imitate what you see.*

## I'll be a monkey's uncle
*I am totally surprised!*

# Monkey Sayings

*And what they mean*

# ANIMAL GAMES

## Monkey in the Middle
a ball, 4 or more players

1.  Choose one player to be the "Monkey," and stand around him or her in a circle.

2.  Throw the ball over the Monkey. The Monkey's goal is to catch the ball, while the group tries to stop him or her.

3.  When the Monkey catches the ball, whoever threw the ball last is the new Monkey and the game starts over.

# Pin the Tail on the Donkey

construction paper, crayons, scissors,
tape, blindfold, 2 or more players

1. Draw a donkey without a tail on a large sheet of construction paper and cut it out. Tape it onto the wall where everybody can reach it.

2. Each player sketches and cuts out a tail on the leftover paper and writes his or her name on it.

Everyone attaches a piece of tape to their tail.

3. One at time blindfold each player and spin him or her around three times. Point the player in the direction of the donkey. Whoever tapes their tail on the donkey (or comes the closest) is the winner!

# Leap Frog
outdoor space, 2 or more players

1. Everybody stands in a straight line.

2. Each player crouches in frog position by bending at the knees. Evenly distribute your weight between your hands and feet. Make sure you all have your heads down.

3. Start with the "frog" at the end of the line. She places her hands on the back of the frog in front of her, and leaps over that person with her legs on either side of him/her. She continues down the line until she's jumped over everybody. Then the new last frog begins jumping, and so on.

# Duck, Duck, Goose

## 4 or more players

1. Choose one player to be "It." Everyone else sits in a circle facing each other.

2. "It" walks around the outside of the circle, tapping each person on the head, calling out the word "Duck." When "It" calls a player "Goose!" that player must get up and chase "It" around the circle and tag "It".

3. If Goose does not tag "It" before "It" makes it all the way around the circle and back into Goose's spot, then Goose becomes "It" and the game starts over. If Goose does catch "It," then Goose gets to sit back in the circle and "It" starts again.

# A TREE TOAD LOVED A SHE-TOAD

A tree toad loved a she-toad
That lived up in a tree.
He was a two-toed tree toad,
But a three-toed toad was she.
The two-toed tree toad tried to win
The three-toed she-toad's heart,
For the two-toed tree toad loved the ground
That the three-toed tree toad trod.
But the two-toed tree toad tried in vain.
He could not please her whim.
In her tree toad bower,
With her three-toed power,
The she-toad vetoed him.

# REPTILE & AMPHIBIAN FACTS

✳ When threatened, the Texas horned lizard will inflate its body, hiss, and squirt blood from its eyes!

✳ The smallest lizard in the world is a species of gecko found in the Virgin Islands. It measures 0.7 inches from snout to hind legs.

✳ Rattlesnakes can shake up to 50 times a minute.

✳ Snakes can smell with their tongues!

✳ By unhinging its jaws, the Komodo dragon can swallow prey up to 4/5 its weight.

✳ Who needs a dentist? Some crocodiles hang around with their mouths open and permit birds to pick pieces of food and parasites from their teeth and gums.

✳ Contrary to popular belief, you cannot tell the age of a rattlesnake by counting its rattles, because it gets a new one every time it sheds its skin, which happens 3 or 4 times a year.

✳ Growing up to 32 feet in length, the reticulated python is believed to be the largest snake in the world.

ut can't hear the sound of their own rattle!

✳ The eyelash viper snake can live for up to a year without eating a meal. How's that for dietary discipline?

✳ The Goliath frog, who lives in the African Congo, can grow to the size of a small cat. That's some *RIBBIT!*

# THE WHITE SNAKE

Long ago in a castle by the Great Sea, lived a powerful King who had many subjects, but only *one* daughter. All the people in his kingdom believed he was the wisest man who ever lived, for their realm was peaceful and the land was rich with bountiful harvests. Men and women traveled from far and wide to seek his council on every matter— from what seeds they should plant in spring to how long winter might last— and he was never wrong. So great were the King's powers that there was nothing— no matter how guarded or secret—that was unknown to him.

But there was one secret that the King kept from all his people—a secret so hidden that even his beloved only daughter did not know. Every night when the Royal Feast was done and the King was alone in the banquet hall, his most loyal young servant brought him a dish covered by a large domed lid. When the King emerged from the hall a few minutes later, his young servant was always waiting to take the dish, still covered, back to its hiding place.

## THE WHITE SNAKE

One morning the King's only daughter arose from bed to find her most prized possession, her dearly departed mother's wedding ring,

missing. A great commotion spread through the castle as everyone, from servants to high court officials, searched in vain for the ring. By late morning the King was convinced that thievery had taken place and all his servants, even his most trusted loyal servant, were under suspicion. Distraught over losing his good standing

with his master, and seeing the King's exquisite only daughter (whom he loved from afar) grief-stricken, the loyal young servant set out to find the thief.

"Who could have stolen the ring," he agonized, "and what will the thief steal next?" Then the loyal young servant had a terrible, bone-chilling thought: "What if the thief stole the King's mysterious dish, too?"

Imagining the blame that would befall him, the young servant dashed to the hiding place of the covered plate and lifted the lid just a crack to make sure its contents remained in place. What he saw astonished him. Beneath the lid, coiled up on the plate, were the remains of a white snake. The young man was mesmerized by the sight. He suddenly felt unable to close the lid or even lift his gaze from the snake's blue

lifeless eyes. Slowly, he felt an irre-
sistible urge to taste it. He struggled
against this magical desire until at last
he ripped off a small piece and ate it.
Instantly, he sensed a change in himself. He began to hear strange noises—
the sounds of many chattering voices
circling him like a breeze. He rushed
to the open window and discovered
that these whispers came from a flock
of birds flying overhead. He could
hear them talking of the great forest
and how they hoped to return there in
the spring. The young servant could
not believe his ears; eating the white
snake remains had given him the
power to understand the language of
animals!

The young servant ran outside
into the courtyard to find out what else
he could hear. As he approached the
pond he heard two wild ducks that
were resting on the banks complaining
to each another.

"Oh, my poor stomach," said the
fatter of the two ducks. "How my
tummy has ached since I gobbled up
that shiny-looking acorn I found on
that castle window ledge."

"The King's only daughter's ring!"
thought the young servant. "That
duck must have eaten it!" Slowly, he
snuck up behind the birds and jumped
out at them, scaring the ducks so
much that the fat one promptly tossed
up her last meal as they flew away in a
flurry of feathers. Sure enough, right
there on the banks where the ducks
had been sitting, lay the King's only
daughter's ring.

The entire castle was overjoyed
when they heard the news that the
loyal young servant had found the
ring. The King himself was so pleased

that he held a special royal banquet that evening and toasted his young servant, declaring that he could have anything he wanted as a reward. When the loyal young servant's gaze met with the sparkling blue eyes of the King's only daughter, he knew right away what he would wish for.

"Your Highness, with your blessing I ask for your daughter's hand in marriage."

The King was dismayed at this request. He could not bear the thought of losing his only daughter. "She is not yet ready to be wed," he protested. "Please, my loyal young servant, you may have anything but that."

The young servant felt his heart sink deep in his chest. "Then I must be released from your service so that I may leave your kingdom. For I cannot look upon her perfect face each day and know that she won't be my bride."

With regret, the King granted his request, and gave him a small bag of gold and a white stallion to aid him in his journey.

Deeply saddened, the loyal young servant set off to find a new life beyond the gates of the castle by the Great Sea. His only comfort was the delight he took in hearing the whispers of the animals he encountered along the way. For weeks he traveled west, following the mighty river that led to the mountains on the edge of the kingdom. One morning, as he mounted his steed, he heard a chorus of tiny voices crying out. It was a colony of ants that were trapped under his stallion's hoofs.

"Darn these humans!" exclaimed the angry Ant King. "Always trampling our homes with their clumsy horses."

# THE WHITE SNAKE

"I am very sorry," replied the young servant. "I shall be more careful in the future."

"Finally," cried the Ant King, "a human with a kind heart. You have made a friend in the ants of this land forever."

So off the young servant rode, following the winding river westward until he once again heard voices crying out. This time it was two little fish caught in the high grass by the riverbank.

"Oh please, someone help us," wailed the tangled fish. "We are caught in the weeds and cannot free ourselves to swim down the river to the Great Sea!"

"I will help you," called out the young servant, and he quickly jumped from his horse and freed the fish from their grassy web.

"Oh, thank you, thank you," chimed the fish. And as the current swept them away down the river, the young servant heard them call out, "You have a friend in us fish for life."

All summer he traveled alone, listening to the chatter of the animals, helping them when he could, and following the river west, until one day he reached the foothills of the mountains on the edge of the kingdom.

"I have traveled a great distance and seen many beautiful things along the way," thought the young servant. "But none can compare with the beauty of the King's only daughter for whom my heart still yearns. Beyond these mountains lies the end of the world. I see now what I must do. I will turn back and beg for the hand of my true love." As he prepared for his long journey home, the young servant heard the whispers of two small baby ravens in distress.

"Our mother has gone to find us food and we fell out of our nest and are not old enough to fly," squeaked the young ravens. "Someone please help us, we are cold and hungry."

The young servant slid off his saddle, scooped up the baby birds, and climbed up the large leafy tree with the ravens carefully tucked under his cloak. When he reached the highest branch he found their nest and gently tucked them back into their beds of twigs and dried leaves.

"Oh, thank you," cooed the young ravens, "you have a friend in the ravens for life."

Winter came swift and hard, and the young servant's journey back down the river was freezing and treacherous. When his steed died one night from the cold he cut up its meat and gave it to starving wolves and wild dogs he encountered along the way. All through the winter he walked alone, following the twisting river back toward the Great Sea. His feet and hands were numb, but his heart ached even more from the pain of lost love.

One morning in the early spring, the young servant finally arrived at the familiar old village below the castle he once called home. There he found all the townspeople gathered in the square. One of the King's courtiers was reading a pronouncement from the King himself.

"It is the spring of my only daughter's twentieth year," read the courtier.

"And though I will mourn the loss of her, I have agreed to allow my daughter to wed. To all the young men of my kingdom, hear this: He who succeeds at the three challenges I have chosen will win my only daughter's hand in marriage. But should you fail at any one of the tasks, death awaits you."

Murmurs could be heard throughout the crowd.

"Agreed to let her wed, has he?" snickered an old beggar woman beside the young servant. "Everyone knows the King will never let his daughter marry. Those three tasks will be impossible. I'm sure of it."

The young men of the town seemed to agree, for not one stepped forth to hear the three challenges.

"Bring me to the castle," called out the young servant, "and I will take the three challenges to win the hand of the King's only daughter."

The crowd parted to let the young servant through and the courtier escorted him through the gates of the castle by the Great Sea.

As he entered the royal court, the King's only daughter gasped and cried out, "Please do not hear these tasks, loyal young servant. You will meet certain death!"

But the King gazed coolly at his former servant and asked him if he was ready to be tested.

"I am ready," said the young servant. But as he looked bravely at the King, his heart beat faster and his hands grew clammy.

"To marry my only daughter you must retrieve three objects," declared the King. "First you must return the ruby ring that I have thrown into the

Great Sea. Second, you must find a single gold seed I have buried in the soil of one of my farmer's fields. And last, you must bring my only daughter an apple from the Tree of Life in the valley beyond the mountains at the end of the world. All this," said the King with a devilish smile, "must be done before tomorrow at dawn, or death will quickly find you."

The court gasped, "These three tasks are impossible. That poor young servant will surely be killed!"

But the young servant was full of hope that he could meet the challenges and wed the King's only daughter, whom he loved with all his heart. He rushed out of the castle and took a boat into the Great Sea to look for the King's ruby ring. The Great Sea was vast and deep, and he did not even know how to swim. Just as the young servant was about to jump headfirst into the dark waters, he heard the whispers of two large fish swimming beside his boat.

"Oh, young servant and friend of the fish, we have heard about your great task and have retrieved the ruby ring from the bottom of the Great Sea. Your kindness to us when we were trapped by the

riverbed will not go unrewarded. Here is the jewel you seek."

Sure enough, the King's ring rested on the fin of one of the fish. The young servant was amazed and thanked them for their help. He quickly sailed back to the kingdom to face the next challenge.

As the sun began to fall below the horizon, the young servant had barely covered a foot of one farmer's field in his search for the golden seed. He started to fear for his life, but still he refused to give in, always picturing the King's only daughter's smiling face. Then, without warning, he heard the whispering of thousands and thousands of tiny ants calling out to each other in a very organized fashion.

"Ant number 5055, what is the report from the third quadrant?"

"Nothing yet, sir," replied a tiny voice from far off.

"And you?" asked another distant ant. "What is your platoon's status in the outer rim?"

"Wait a minute, sir," cried yet another wee voice. "The Ant King has just informed me that the seed has been found. I repeat, the seed has been found!"

A chorus of cheers rose up from the ground, and before the young servant knew it, the Ant King presented him with the King's gold seed.

"Good luck, friend of the ants," said the Ant King. "May your third task go as well."

The young servant thanked him and dashed off toward the long river, which flowed to the mountains at the end of the world, beyond which was the valley that held the Tree of Life.

By now it had grown dark, and the young servant was out of breath from running as fast as his tired legs could carry him. Although he knew that it had taken him two seasons on horseback to make it up the river, he decided not to give up. Never in his young life had he ever wanted something so much. He was prepared to die trying to bring an apple from the Tree of Life to the King's only daughter.

As the night grew cold and the moon began to wane, the young servant could run no more. His body collapsed under a tree by the riverbed. Just as he closed his eyes to pray for strength to continue, he heard the whisper of two ravens calling to him from the night sky above.

"Friend of the ravens," they said, "you saved our lives when we were young and now we are returning the good deed." Into his hands fell a shiny golden apple freshly plucked from the Tree of Life.

"Now run loyal young servant, run fast. For there is not much night left, and your journey back will be long."

With renewed hope and strength the young servant raced toward home clutching the ring, the seed, and the apple in his cloak. For hours he ran in the dark, guided only by the sounds of the rushing river that led to the Great Sea and the castle beside it. An hour before dawn, he had only one mile left to go. But he was so tired he could not take another step. In a feverish state he tried to crawl a few feet before total exhaustion set in and he fell into a deep sleep.

The morning sun had still not shown itself when the young servant felt his body being slowly dragged through the farmers' fields and past the sleeping village. He barely noticed the many small paws and mouths gently

# THE WHITE SNAKE

pulling him up the road that led to the castle gates. All the animals that he had helped during his travels silently dragged him across the drawbridge and into the King's courtyard. The wolves and wild dogs began to howl, the birds chirped, and the frogs croaked, waking the entire castle just before the break of dawn. When the King looked out his royal window and heard the animals tell of the servant's good deeds, his heart warmed to the young man and he gladly accepted him as his future son-in-law.

The news of the young servant's success spread quickly throughout the kingdom, and all the townspeople took to the streets to celebrate. Everyone agreed that this was a truly blessed union, for it had brought together not only two young lovers, but all the people and animals of the land.

And so it was that on the day of their wedding the newlyweds shared a bite from the Tree of Life's apple and lived happily ever after as husband and wife.

# PIPING PETER

BY LILIAN HOLMES

When through the grass
Shy creatures pass,
And wild things steal from cover—
When round their nests,
In leafy crests,
The gentle ring-doves hover—
When, leaving rosy trails behind,
And all the copse in gloaming,
The sun sinks in the west,
  you'll find
Peter the Piper roaming:
And he pipes so soft,
And he pipes so low,
No timid creature fears him;

But bird and beast,
With eyes aglow,
Creep closer yet to hear him.
Beneath the magic of his spell
Soon, soon, they will be falling—
Hark! A thrush cries, "*Hush, sweet,
  hurry, come along—
Peter the Piper's calling!*"
And music floats,
In fluty notes,
Through branches softly swaying—
Is it redbreast, nightingale,
Bullfinch, thrush,
Or Peter the Piper playing?

# BLACK BEAUTY

## BY ANNA SEWELL

*Named for its main character,* Black Beauty *tells the story of a horse's long and varied life, from a well-born colt in a pleasant meadow to an overworked cab horse. In this chapter, an older and frailer Black Beauty finds himself up for sale yet again.*

At this sale, of course, I found myself in company with the old broken-down horses—some lame, some broken-winded, some old, and some that I am sure it would have been merciful to shoot.

The buyers and sellers too, many of them, looked not much better off than the poor beasts they were bargaining about. There were poor old men, trying to get a horse or pony for a few pounds, that might drag about some little wood or coal cart. There were poor men trying to sell a worn-out beast for two or three pounds, rather than have the greater loss of killing him. Some of them looked as if poverty and hard times had hardened them all over; but there were others that I would have willingly used the last of my strength in serving; poor and shabby, but kind and human, with voices that I could trust. There was one tottering old man that took a great fancy to me, and I to him, but I was not strong enough—it was an anxious time!

# BLACK BEAUTY

Coming from a better part of the fair, I noticed a man who looked like a gentleman farmer, with a young boy by his side; he had a broad back and round shoulders, a kind, ruddy face, and he wore a broad-brimmed hat. When he came up to me and my companions, he stood still, and gave a pitiful look round upon us. I saw his eye rest on me; I had still a good mane and tail, which did something for my appearance. I pricked my ears and looked at him.

"There's a horse, Willie, that has known better days."

"Poor old fellow!" said the boy, "do you think, grandpapa, he was ever a carriage horse?"

"Oh, yes, my boy," said the farmer coming closer, "he might have been anything when he was young; look at his nostrils and his ears, the shape of his neck and shoulder; there's a deal of breeding about that horse." He put out his hand and gave me a kind pat on the neck. I put out my nose in answer to his kindness; the boy stroked my face.

"Poor old fellow! see, grandpapa, how well he understands kindness. Could not you buy him and make him young again, as you did with Ladybird?"

"My dear boy, I can't make all old horses young; besides, Ladybird was not so very old, as she was run down and badly used."

"Well, grandpapa, I don't believe that this one is old; look at his mane and tail. I wish you would look into his mouth, and then you could tell; though he is so very thin, his eyes are not sunk like some old horses'."

The old gentleman laughed. "Bless the boy! he is as horsey as his old grandfather."

"But do look at his mouth, grand-papa, and ask the price; I am sure he would grow young in our meadows."

The man who had brought me for sale now put in his word.

"The young gentleman's a real knowing one, sir; now the fact is, this 'ere hoss is just pulled down with over-work in the cabs; he's not an old one, and I heerd as how the vetenary should say, that a six months' run off would set him right up, being as how his wind was not broken. I've had the tending of him these ten days past, and a gratefuller, pleasanter animal I never met with, and 'twould be worth a gentleman's while to give a five-pound note for him, and let him have a chance. I'll be bound he'd be worth twenty pounds next spring."

The old gentleman laughed, and the little boy looked up eagerly.

"Oh! grandpapa, did you not say the colt sold for five pounds more than you expected? You would not be poorer if you did buy this one."

The farmer slowly felt my legs, which were much swelled and strained; then he looked at my mouth: "Thirteen or fourteen, I should say; just trot him out, will you?"

I arched my poor thin neck, raised my tail a little, and threw out my legs as well as I could, for they were very stiff.

# BLACK BEAUTY

"What is the lowest you will take for him?" said the farmer as I came back.

"Five pounds, sir; that was the lowest price my master set."

"'Tis a speculation," said the old gentleman, shaking his head, but at the same time slowly drawing out his purse—"quite a speculation! Have you any more business here?" he said, counting the sovereigns into his hand.

"No, sir, I can take him for you to the inn, if you please."

"Do so, I am now going there."

They walked forward, and I was led behind. The boy could hardly control his delight, and the old gentleman seemed to enjoy his pleasure. I had a good feed at the inn, and was then gently ridden home by a servant of my new master's and turned into a large meadow with a shed in one corner of it.

Mr. Thoroughgood, for that was the name of my benefactor, gave orders that I should have hay and oats every night and morning, and the run of the meadow during the day, and, "You, Willie," said he, "must take the oversight of him; I give him in charge to you."

The boy was proud of his charge, and undertook it in all seriousness. There was not a day when he did not pay me a visit; sometimes picking me out from amongst the other horses, and giving me a bit of carrot, or something good, or sometimes standing by me whilst I ate my oats. He always came with kind words and caresses, and of course I grew very fond of him. He called me Old Crony, as I used to come to him in the field and follow him about. Sometimes he brought his grandfather, who always looked closely at my legs:

"This is our point, Willie," he would say; "but he is improving so steadily that I think we shall see a change for the better in the spring."

The perfect rest, the good food, the soft turf, and gentle exercise, soon began to tell on my condition and my spirits. I had a good constitution from my mother, and I was never strained when I was young, so that I had a better chance than many horses, who have been worked before they came to their full strength. During the winter my legs improved so much that I began to feel quite young again. The spring came round, and one day in March Mr. Thoroughgood determined that he would try me in the phaeton. I was well pleased, and he and Willie drove me a few miles. My legs were not stiff now and I did the work with perfect ease.

"He's growing young, Willie; we must give him a little gentle work now, and by midsummer he will be as good as Ladybird; he has a beautiful mouth, and good paces, they can't be better."

"Oh! grandpapa, how glad I am you bought him!"

"So am I, my boy, but he has to thank you more than me; we must now be looking out for a quiet genteel place for him, where he will be valued."

You can lead a horse to water

but you can't make him drink

# Horse Sayings

*And what they mean*

## Don't change horses in midstream

*If you start something, see it through.*

## If wishes were horses then beggars would ride

*Wishing doesn't make things happen.*

## Putting the cart before the horse

*Getting ahead of yourself.*

# Don't look a gift horse in the mouth

*Be grateful for any present you receive, even if it's not exactly what you wanted.*

# Straight out of the horse's mouth

*Directly from the original source.*

## *THE DOG*
### BY OGDEN NASH

The truth I do not stretch or shove
When I state the dog is full of love.
I've also proved, by actual test,
A wet dog is the lovingest.

*A True Story*

# MAN'S BEST FRIEND

*BY SARA BAYSINGER*

In 1858, shepherd John Gray was laid to rest in Greyfriars Churchyard, Edinburgh's oldest cemetery. Among the mourners who gathered there was Gray's faithful Skye terrier, Bobby. No one had the heart that day—or in the days that followed—to point out the "no dogs allowed" decree posted on the churchyard gates. So Greyfriars Bobby, as he came to be known, was permitted to stand watch over his master's grave.

For the next fourteen years, until his own death, Bobby was never far from the churchyard. Concerned neighbors tried to bring the pup indoors during bad weather, but he would howl until he was let out to go back to his duty. Once a day, Bobby did leave his post. At one o'clock, he would trot over to collect his bone at the local inn—the same inn where for years, John Gray took his one o'clock lunch while Bobby chewed a bone at his feet.

Locals were moved by Bobby's unwavering loyalty. They gave him treats and built a little house for him on the church grounds. The groundskeeper personally paid the dog's license fee, and Bobby was given a collar so he wouldn't be mistaken for a stray.

The touching story of the little dog's devotion spread far and wide. Visitors came to the churchyard especially to see the constant canine from the Isle of Skye. Shortly after his death, a bronze statue of Greyfriars Bobby was placed near the cemetery gates. He is now buried within the churchyard, close to his master forever.

# Oh Where, oh Where Has My Little Dog Gone

Oh where, oh where has my lit - tle dog gone? Oh

where, oh where can he be? _____ With his

ears cut short and his tail cut long; oh

where, oh where can he be? Oh

where, oh where has my lit - tle dog gone? Oh

where, oh where can he be? _____ With his

ears cut short and his tail cut long; oh

where, oh where can he be?

## FUZZY WUZZY

Fuzzy Wuzzy was a bear,
Fuzzy Wuzzy had no hair,
Fuzzy Wuzzy wasn't fuzzy,
Was he?

# BABY ANIMAL FACTS

✳ A baby panda is born hairless and blind,
and weighs only about 3 to 5 ounces.

✳ The quills of a porcupine are soft and pliable at birth, but begin to harden within an hour.

✳ An elephant calf weighs appro

✳ Baby orangutans continue to breastfeed for nearly 3 years
and live with their mothers until they are about 7 years old.

✳ Many crocodile mothers carry their hatchlings
protectively in their mouths when they take them
from the nest to the water.

✳ When it first hatches, a chick will follow the first moving object it sees,
thinking it is their parent. This event is called imprinting.

✳ A kangaroo is only 1 inch long at birth.

Just as we humans refer to our infant offspring as "babies," we also have names for the offspring of animals. Here are the "baby" names for a variety of different species.

| ANIMAL | BABY NAME | ANIMAL | BABY NAME |
|---|---|---|---|
| Alligator | hatchling | Goose | gosling |
| Ape | baby | Grasshopper | nymph |
| Bat | pup | Horse | foal (male), filly (female) |
| Bear | cub | Jellyfish | ephyna |

# mately 300 pounds at birth.

| ANIMAL | BABY NAME | ANIMAL | BABY NAME |
|---|---|---|---|
| Bee | larva | Hippo | calf |
| Cat | kitten | Kangaroo | joey |
| Chicken | chick | Llama | cria |
| Cow | calf | Mouse | pinkie |
| Deer | fawn | Owl | owlet |
| Dog | puppy | Oyster | spat |
| Duck | duckling | Pigeon | squab |
| Eagle | eaglet | Rabbit | bunny |
| Fish | fry, fingerling | Sheep | lamb, lambkin |
| Fly | maggot | Swan | cygnet, flapper |
| Fox | kit | Whale | calf |
| Frog | tadpole, pollywog | Wolf | whelp |
| Goat | kid | Zebra | colt |

# THE ELEPHANT'S CHILD

### By Rudyard Kipling

In the High and Far-Off Times the Elephant, O Best Beloved, had no trunk. He had only a blackish, bulgy nose, as big as a boot, that he could wriggle about from side to side; but he couldn't pick up things with it. But there was one Elephant—a new Elephant—an Elephant's Child—who was full of 'satiable curiosity, and that means he asked ever so many questions. *And* he lived in Africa, and he filled all Africa with his 'satiable curtiosities. He asked his tall aunt, the Ostrich, why her tail-feathers grew just so, and his tall aunt, the Ostrich, spanked him with her hard, hard claw. He asked his tall uncle, the Giraffe, what made his skin spotty, and his tall uncle, the Giraffe, spanked him with his hard, hard hoof. And still he was full of 'satiable curtiosity! He asked his broad aunt, the Hippopotamus, why her eyes were red, and his broad aunt, the Hippopotamus, spanked him with her broad, broad hoof; and he asked his hairy uncle, the Baboon, why melons tasted just so, and his hairy uncle, the Baboon, spanked him with his hairy, hairy paw. And *still* he was full of 'satiable curtiosity! He asked questions

93

about everything that he saw, or heard, or felt, or smelt, or touched, and all his uncles and his aunts spanked him. And still he was full of 'satiable curtiosity!

One fine morning in the middle of the Precession of the Equinoxes this 'satiable Elephant's Child asked a new fine question that he had never asked before. He asked, 'What does the Crocodile have for dinner?' Then everybody said, 'Hush!' in a loud and dretful tone, and they spanked him immediately and directly, without stopping, for a long time.

By and by, when that was finished, he came upon Kolokolo Bird sitting in the middle of a wait-a-bit thorn-bush, and he said, 'My father has spanked me, and my mother has spanked me; all my aunts and uncles have spanked me for my 'satiable curtiosity; and *still* I want to know what the Crocodile has for dinner!'

Then Kolokolo Bird said, with a mournful cry, 'Go to the banks of the great grey-green, greasy Limpopo River, all set about with fever-trees, and find out.'

That very morning, when there was nothing left of the Equinoxes, because the Precession had preceded according to precedent, this 'satiable Elephant's Child took a hundred pounds of bananas (the little short red kind), and a hundred pounds of sugar-cane (the long purple kind), and seventeen melons (the greeny-crackly kind), and said to all his dear families, 'Good-bye. I am going to the great grey-green, greasy Limpopo River, all set about with fever-trees, to find out what the Crocodile has for dinner.' And they all spanked him once more for luck, though he asked them most politely to stop.

## THE ELEPHANT'S CHILD

Then he went away, a little warm, but not at all astonished, eating melons, and throwing the rind about, because he could not pick it up.

He went from Graham's Town to Kimberley, and from Kimberley to Khama's Country, and from Khama's Country he went east by north, eating melons all the time, till at last he came to the banks of the great grey-green, greasy Limpopo River, all set about with fever-trees, precisely as Kolokolo Bird had said.

Now you must know and understand, O Best Beloved, that till that very week, and day, and hour, and minute, this 'satiable Elephant's Child had never seen a Crocodile, and did not know what one was like. It was all his 'satiable curtiosity.

The first thing that he found was a Bi-Coloured-Python-Rock-Snake curled around a rock.

"Scuse me,' said the Elephant's Child most politely, 'but have you seen such a thing as a Crocodile in these promiscuous parts?'

'*Have* I seen a Crocodile?' said the Bi-Coloured-Python-Rock-Snake, in a voice of dretful scorn. 'What will you ask me next?'

"Scuse me,' said the Elephant's Child, 'but could you kindly tell me what he has for dinner?'

Then the Bi-Coloured-Python-Rock-Snake uncoiled himself very quickly from the rock, and spanked the Elephant's Child with his scalesome, flailsome tail.

# THE ELEPHANT'S CHILD

'That is odd,' said the Elephant's Child, 'because my father and my mother, and my uncle, and my aunt, not to mention my other aunt, the Hippopotamus, and my other uncle, the Baboon, have all spanked me for my 'satiable curtiosity—and I suppose this is the same thing.'

So he said good-bye very politely to the Bi-Coloured-Python-Rock-Snake, and helped to coil him up on the rock again, and went on, a little warm, but not at all astonished, eating melons, and throwing the rind about, because he could not pick it up, till he trod on what he thought was a log of wood at the very edge of the great grey-green, greasy Limpopo River, all set about with fever-trees.

But it was really the Crocodile, O Best Beloved, and the Crocodile winked one eye—like this!

''Scuse me,' said the Elephant's Child most politely, 'but do you happen to have seen a Crocodile in these promiscuous parts?'

Then the Crocodile winked the other eye, and lifted half his tail out of the mud; and the Elephant's Child stepped back most politely, because he did not wish to be spanked again.

'Come hither, Little One,' said the Crocodile. 'Why do you ask such things?'

''Scuse me,' said the Elephant's Child most politely, 'but my father has spanked me, my mother has spanked me, not to mention my tall aunt, the Ostrich, and my tall uncle, the Giraffe, who can kick ever so had, as well as my broad aunt, the Hippopotamus, and my hairy uncle, the Baboon, *and* including the

# THE ELEPHANT'S CHILD

Bi-Coloured-Python-Rock-Snake, with the scalesome, flailsome tail, just up the bank, who spanks harder than any of them; and *so*, if it's quite all the same to you, I don't want to be spanked any more.'

'Come hither, Little One,' said the Crocodile, 'for I am the Crocodile,' and he wept crocodile-tears to show it was quite true.

Then the Elephant's Child grew all breathless, and panted, and kneeled down on the bank and said, 'You are the very person I have been looking for all these long days. Will you please tell me what you have for dinner?'

'Come hither, Little One,' said the Crocodile, 'and I'll whisper.'

Then the Elephant's Child put his head down close to the Crocodile's musky, tusky mouth, and the Crocodile caught him by his little nose, which up to that very week, day, hour, and minute, had been no bigger than a boot, though much more useful.

'I think,' said the Crocodile—and he said it between his teeth, like this— 'I think to-day I will begin with Elephant's Child!'

At this, O Best Beloved, the Elephant's Child was much annoyed, and he said, speaking through his nose, like this, 'Led go! You are hurtig be!'

Then the Bi-Coloured-Python-Rock-Snake scuffled down from the bank and said, 'My young friend, if you do not now, immediately and instantly, pull as hard as ever you can, it is my opinion that your acquaintance in the large-pattern leather ulster' (and by this he meant the Crocodile) 'will jerk you into yonder limpid stream before you can say Jack Robinson.'

# THE ELEPHANT'S CHILD

This is the way Bi-Coloured-Python-Rock-Snakes always talk.

Then the Elephant's Child sat back on his little haunches, and pulled, and pulled, and pulled, and his nose began to stretch. And the Crocodile floundered into the water, making it all creamy with great sweeps of his tail, and *he* pulled, and pulled, and pulled.

And the Elephant's Child's nose kept on stretching; and the Elephant's Child spread all his little four legs and pulled, and pulled, and pulled, and his nose kept on stretching; and the Crocodile threshed his tail like an oar, and *he* pulled, and pulled, and pulled, and at each pull the Elephant's Child's nose grew longer and longer—and it hurt him *hijjus*!

Then the Elephant's Child felt his legs slipping, and he said through his nose, which was now nearly five feet long, 'This is too butch for be!'

Then the Bi-Coloured-Python-Rock-Snake came down from the bank, and knotted himself in a double-clove-hitch round the Elephant's Child's hind legs, and said, 'Rash and inexperienced traveller, we will now seriously devote ourselves to a little high tension, because if we do not, it is my impression that yonder self-propelling man-of-war with the armour-plated upper deck' (and by this, O Best Beloved, he meant the Crocodile), 'will permanently vitiate your future career.'

That is the way all Bi-Coloured-Python-Rock-Snakes always talk.

So he pulled, and the Elephant's Child pulled, and the Crocodile pulled; but the Elephant's Chld and the Bi-Coloured-Python-Rock-Snake pulled hardest; and at last the Crocodile let go

98

of the Elephant's Child's nose with a plop that you could hear all up and down the Limpopo.

Then the Elephant's Child sat down most hard and sudden; but first he was careful to say 'Thank you' to the Bi-Coloured-Python-Rock-Snake; and next he was kind to his poor pulled nose, and wrapped it all up in cool banana leaves, and hung it in the great grey-green, greasy Limpopo to cool.

'What are you doing that for?' said the Bi-Coloured-Python-Rock-Snake.

"Scuse me,' said the Elephant's Child, 'but my nose is badly out of shape, and I am waiting for it to shrink.'

'Then you will have to wait a long time,' said the Bi-Coloured-Python-Rock-Snake. 'Some people do not know what is good for them.'

The Elephant's Child sat there for three days waiting for his nose to shrink. But it never grew any shorter, and, besides, it made him squint.

At the end of the third day, a fly came and stung him on the shoulder, and before he knew what he was doing he lifted up his trunk and hit that fly dead with the end of it.

"Vantage number one!' said the Bi-Coloured-Python-Rock-Snake. 'You couldn't have done that with a mere-smear nose. Try and eat a little now.'

Before he thought what he was doing the Elephant's Child put out his trunk and plucked a large bundle of grass, dusted it clean against his fore-legs, and stuffed it into his own mouth.

"Vantage number two!' said the Bi-Coloured-Python-Rock-Snake. 'You couldn't have done that with a mere-smear nose. Don't you think the sun is very hot here?'

'It is,' said the Elephant's Child, and before he thought what he was doing he schlooped up a schloop of mud from the banks of the great grey-green, greasy Limpopo, and slapped it on his head, where it made a cool schloopy-sloshy mud-cap all trickly behind his ears.

"Vantage number three!' said the Bi-Coloured-Python-Rock-Snake. 'You couldn't have done that with a mere-smear nose. Now how do you feel about being spanked again?'

"Scuse me,' said the Elephant's Child, 'but I should not like it at all.'

'How would you like to spank somebody?' said the Bi-Coloured-Python-Rock-Snake.

'I should like it very much indeed,' said the Elephant's Child.

'Well,' said the Bi-Coloured-Python-Rock-Snake, 'you will find that new nose of yours very useful to spank people with.'

'Thank you,' said the Elephant's Child, 'I'll remember that; and now I think I'll go home to all my dear families and try.'

So the Elephant's Child went home across Africa frisking and whisking his trunk. He went especially out of his way to find a broad Hippopotamus (she was no relation of his), and he spanked her very hard, to make sure that the Bi-Coloured-Python-Rock-Snake had spoken the truth about his new trunk. The rest of the time he picked up the melon rinds that he had dropped on his way to the Limpopo—for he was a Tidy Pachyderm.

One dark evening he came back to all his dear families, and he coiled up his trunk and said, 'How do you do?'

They were very glad to see him, and immediately said, 'Come here and be spanked for your 'satiable curtiosity.'

'Pooh,' said the Elephant's Child. 'I don't think you peoples know anything about spanking; but *I* do, and I'll show you.'

Then he uncurled his trunk and knocked two of his dear brothers head over heels.

'O Bananas!' said they, 'where did you learn that trick, and what have you done to your nose?'

'I got a new one from the Crocodile on the banks of the great grey-green, greasy Limpopo River,' said the Elephant's Child. 'I asked him what he had for dinner, and he gave me this to keep.'

'It looks very ugly,' said his hairy uncle, the Baboon.

'It does,' said the Elephant's Child. 'But it's very useful.' Then that bad Elephant's Child spanked all his dear families for a long time, till they were very warm and greatly astonished.

At last things grew so exciting that his dear families went off one by one in a hurry to the banks of the great grey-green, greasy Limpopo River, all set about with fever-trees, to borrow new noses from the Crocodile. When they came back nobody spanked anybody any more; and ever since that day, O Best Beloved, all the Elephants you will ever see, besides all those that you won't, have trunks precisely like the trunk of the 'satiable Elephant's Child.

# ELETELEPHONY

## BY LAURA E. RICHARDS

Once there was an elephant,
Who tried to use the telephant—
No! No! I mean an elephone
Who tried to use the telephone—
(Dear me! I am not certain quite
That even now I've got it right.)

Howe'er it was, he got his trunk
Entangled in the telephunk;
The more he tried to get it free,
The louder buzzed the telephee—
(I fear I'd better drop the song
Of elephop and telephong!)

**1.**

**2.**

**3.**

# Animal
# Letter Game

Look closely at these animal drawings—can you see they're made from the letters that spell the animal's name? Identify the critter each letter drawing depicts. Once you've guessed them all correctly, try to make up some drawings of your own. If you like, go ahead and add an extra line, squiggle, or dot to complete your picture.

**4.**

**5.**

**6.**

**Answers:** 1. Cat. 2. Elephant 3. Dog, 4. Horse, 5. Vulture. 6. Cow 7. Crow, 8. Pig, 9. Cat

**7.**

**8.**

**9.**

# ANIMAL PANCAKES

**O**n that rainy day when you can't get to the zoo, make one at home with this recipe for animal pancakes. Chew on a monkey, slurp up a snake, and soak that elephant in a big puddle of syrup. Here's how:

1½ cups unbleached white flour

1 tablespoon sugar

¼ tablespoon salt

1 tablespoon baking powder

3 eggs, separated

¼ cup melted butter (easily done in the microwave)

2 cups milk

1. Preheat oven to 200°F and put a plate in to warm.

2. In a large bowl, combine dry ingredients.

3. In another bowl, beat egg yolks with the melted butter and milk. Stir into the flour mixture.

4. Beat egg whites until they are fluffy and fold them into the batter.

5. Heat a lightly buttered frying pan over medium-high heat.

6. Using a spouted cup or bowl, pour batter onto the griddle in the shape of your child's favorite animal. When the bubbles start to dry, flip and brown on the other side.

7. Use a raisin, blueberry, nut or chocolate chip to make the animal's eye.

8. Keep pancakes warm in the oven until ready to serve.

9. Butter lightly and drizzle with syrup. Serve warm.

*Serves four to six*

# NOAH'S ARK

### GENESIS 6-8

Many, many years passed since Adam and Eve had left Eden. They had had lots of children, and now had grandchildren, great grandchildren, and great great grandchildren! God hoped the offspring of Adam and Eve would respect the earth and care for the animals, but it turned out they did no such thing. Instead, these people became mean and selfish, and often acted in horrible ways. They had stopped listening to God.

"I'm sorry I ever created these people," God said sadly. "I shall start over and destroy the world."

But first he went to see a man named Noah.

Noah was six hundred years old and had three sons, Shem, Ham, and Jepheth. Noah was kind and honest, and he always obeyed God.

"Noah," God said, when he found him, "I plan to cause a huge flood to wash over the earth. Everyone will drown—except for you and your family and some animals."

Noah listened carefully as God told him what to do.

"Build an ark of wood with large

108

# NOAH'S ARK

rooms inside, and be sure to seal all the cracks with pitch to keep the water out," God instructed. Then he gave him the exact measurements of the wood. "It will have three decks, a window near the top, and a door on the side.

"When the seas begin to rise, this ark will be a safe place for you and your wife, your three sons and their wives."

"I'll do as you say," Noah said, grateful that he and his family were to be spared.

"But why do we need such a large ark?"

"Because you are to bring with you two of each living creature, one male and one female, so that they can multiply in the new world. And you'll need lots of food, too."

Noah rounded up his sons and they got right to work. They measured and hammered, sawed and sanded, and soon the ark began to take shape.

"What a stupid thing to make," a neighbor said to Noah.

"What do you expect from such a crazy old man?" said another neighbor.

But Noah didn't listen to any of them. He listened only to God.

When the ark was finally finished, Noah and his sons rounded up the animals. Then, at last, they were ready to board the ark.

First, Noah led his family up the wooden plank that led to the highest deck. Next came the animals, two by two. *Grrrrrr. Grrrrr. Cluck. Cluck. Stomp. Stomp. Quack. Quack. Ruff. Ruff. Neigh. Neigh. Tweet. Tweet. Squeak! Squeak! Mooo! Mooo! Wh-ish. Wh-ish. Cheep. Cheep. Snort. Snort. Oink. Oink. Hiss! Hiss! Meow! Meow!*

Hyenas, goats, peacocks, zebras, turtles, camels, giraffes, doves, hippopotami, pheasants, bears, penguins, donkeys, lizards, rabbits, frogs, buffalo, sheep, and every other animal imaginable climbed aboard with its mate. Some had spots, some were striped, some were huge, some were tiny, some were loud, some were quiet. What a magnificent parade!

"They'll never be able to drag that boat to the sea," a neighbor said, having no idea about the floods. "It's much too heavy." The other neighbors laughed.

Just as Noah and his sons pulled up the wooden plank, the sky grew cloudy. Then it began to sprinkle.

By the time they showed the pigs to their sty near the middle deck, the horses to their stables near the upper deck, the chickens to their coops near the front of the ark, the kittens to their basket near the back of the ark, and the other animals to their own special areas, the rain had started coming down.

*Pitter-patter, pitter-patter.* The drops splattered against the shutters of the window near the top of the boat. *Pitter-patter, pitter-patter.* The drops splattered against the window shutters of a nearby house where people were pushing and shoving for a place to look out. They all wanted to watch the ark as puddles formed around it.

B-O-OOM! Thunder crashed. Lightning flashed. The rain pounded and poured as the wind picked up strength and speed. On land, roofs began to leak, puddles poured into other puddles, and people grew frantic. Noah's ark no longer seemed like such a bad idea to them. For forty days and forty nights, it rained and poured. Puddles became rivers and rivers became seas. The ark tossed and turned as giant waves crashed thousands of feet in the air! The last of the rooftops and treetops and mountaintops had long since dis-

# NOAH'S ARK

appeared beneath the floods. But Noah, his family, and the animals were safe and dry inside the ark.

At the end of the fortieth day, the rain suddenly stopped. Everything was silent and still, and the ark rocked gently in the water. Noah hurried to the window and gasped. All he saw was water—water everywhere. Not a house or tree or mountain in sight! "God has done what he set out to do," he announced to the others. "The old world is gone forever!"

Then he beckoned to a raven. The raven left its mate and flew over to Noah.

"Fly out to look for dry land," Noah said to the raven. "When you find it, come back and show us the way."

After the raven flew out the window, Noah flung open the door and led his wife, and then his sons and their wives, onto the upper deck of the ark. Next came two panthers, then two pandas, then two crocodiles, two blue jays, and two swans. Soon all three decks were completely full!

It had been so long since they had been outside, and the fresh air felt wonderful! Two days later the raven returned. It looked tired and hungry— and it hadn't found an inch of land. It hadn't even found a place to perch! Next, Noah sent out a dove. The dove was gone for many months and finally returned with an olive leaf in its beak.

"The water must be going down!" Noah said. "The land is finally drying up!"

After a hearty meal and a good night's cuddle with its mate, the dove flew out again. While it was gone, the waters

# NOAH'S ARK

got lower and lower until small islands, and then larger pieces of land, began to poke through. This time, the dove didn't return—but no one seemed to mind.

"It's time to leave the ark," God said to Noah one day. "Bring your wife and your sons and their wives, and bring every pair of animals so they can have lots of babies. Welcome to the new world!"

When they drifted onto land, Noah and his sons set up the wooden plank and two by two the animals left the ark. The tigers prowled down the plank. The chickens scrambled down the plank. The elephants climbed down the plank. The ducks waddled down the plank. The puppies scurried down the plank. The horses galloped down the plank. The canaries fluttered down the plank. The mice scampered down the plank.

The cows roamed down the plank. The worms wiggled down the plank. The monkeys swung down the plank. The bulls charged down the plank. The pigs scuffled down the plank. The snakes slithered down the plank. The kittens pattered down the plank. And all the other animals followed behind them.

Next came Noah's sons and their wives.

And last, Noah and his wife came down the plank. It felt strange to walk on dry land, for they had been on the ark for so long!

Noah and his family sat on the ground and thanked God for taking care of them.

When God heard their thanks, he gave them a beautiful gift in the sky— a dazzling rainbow, the first ever.

113

# THE UNICORN

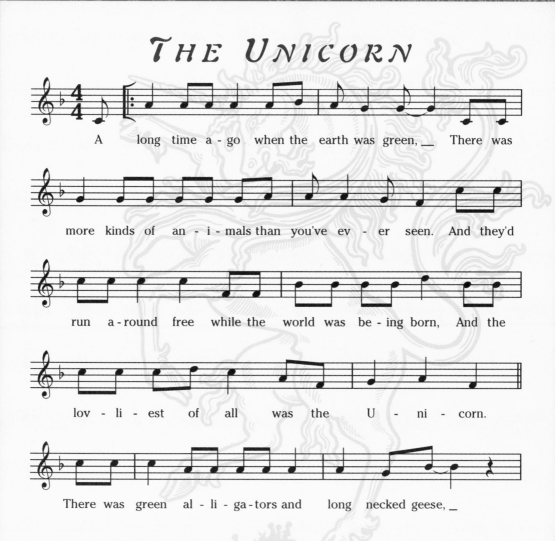

A long time a-go when the earth was green, __ There was

more kinds of an - i - mals than you've ev - er seen. And they'd

run a - round free while the world was be - ing born, And the

lov - li - est of all was the U - ni - corn.

There was green al - li - ga-tors and long necked geese, __

Hump back cam - els and chim - pan - zees, ____

Cats and rats and e - le - phants but sure as you're born, __ The

lov - li - est of all was the U - ni - corn.

*Piano solo*

*Sing:*

But the U - ni - corn.

2. But the Lord seen some sinnin'
　　　and it caused him pain,
He says, "Stand back, I'm gonna make it rain.
So hey, Brother Noah, I'll tell you what to do,
Go and build me a floating zoo."

CHORUS:
"And you take two alligators and a couple of geese,
Two hump back camels and two chimpanzees,
Two cats, two rats, two elephants,
　　　but sure as you're born,
Noah, don't you forget my unicorns."

3. Now Noah was there and he answered the callin',
And he finished up the ark as the rain started fallin',
Then he marched in the animals two by two,
And he sung out as they went through:

CHORUS:
"Hey Lord, I got you two alligators
　　　and a couple of geese,
Two hump back camels and two chimpanzees,
Two cats, two rats, two elephants,
　　　but sure as you're born,
Lord, I just don't see your unicorns."

4. Well, Noah looked out through the drivin' rain,
But the unicorns was hidin'—playin' silly games,
They were kickin' and a-splashin'
　　　while the rain was pourin',
Oh them foolish unicorns.

CHORUS: Repeat 2nd Chorus.

5. Then the ducks started duckin' and the snakes
　　　started snakin',
And the elephants started elephantin' and the boat
　　　started shakin',
The mice started squeakin' and the lions
　　　started roarin',
And everyone's aboard but them unicorns.

CHORUS:
I mean the two alligators and a couple of geese,
The hump back camels and the chimpanzees,
Noah cried, "Close the door 'cause the rain is pourin',
And we just can't wait for them unicorns."

6. And then the ark started movin'
　　　and it drifted with tide,
And the unicorns looked up from the rock and cried,
And the water came up and sort of floated them away,
That's why you've never seen a unicorn to this day.

CHORUS:
You'll see a lot of alligators and a whole mess of geese,
You'll see hump back camels and chimpanzees,
You'll see cats and rats and elephants but sure
　　　as you're born,
You're never gonna see no unicorn.

# MYTHICAL ANIMALS

✳ A serpent that has the upper body of a rooster
and the lower body of a snake is called a cockatrice.
It can kill with just a glance.

✳ Werewolves are humans that change into wolves in the presence of a full moon.
According to legend, there are many ways a person can become a werewolf. One belief
was that the werewolf curse is hereditary and could be passed from parent to child, while
another theory claimed you must be bitten by a werewolf to turn into one yourself.

✳ The snakelike basilisk can murder with its breath or the touch
of its tale. The sight of its own reflection brings instant death.

✳ A gryphon is a powerful beast with the body

✳ The Chinese dragon is said to be made up of the body parts of nine
different creatures: The head of a camel, the eyes of a demon, the ears of a
cow, the horns of a stag, the neck of a snake, the belly of a clam, the claws
of an eagle, the soles of the feet of a tiger, and the scales of a carp.

✳ A unicorn is an exotic white horse with a single horn in the center of its head. These elusive animals are believed to be quite magical, and are rarely glimpsed by man. It is thought that the unicorn's horn alone may hold the power to purify water and counteract poison.

✳ The Phoenix is the legendary bird of fire. It is said that it lives for five hundred years. As this mighty winged creature approaches its time of death, it builds itself a nest and lights itself on fire. As it burns, a new phoenix is born and rises from the flames and ash. Only one phoenix can exist at a time.

of a lion and the head and wings of an eagle.

✳ The Minotaur is described in Greek mythology as having the body of a man and the head of a bull. Imprisoned in a labyrinth by the son of Zeus, the Minotaur survived on a steady diet of young children who had the misfortune of getting lost in its maze.

# HOW THE CAMEL GOT HIS HUMP

### BY RUDYARD KIPLING

Now this is the next tale, and it tells how the Camel got his big hump.

In the beginning of years, when the world was so new-and-all, and the Animals were just beginning to work for Man, there was a Camel, and he lived in the middle of a Howling Desert because he did not want to work; and besides, he was a Howler himself. So he ate sticks and thorns and tamarisks and milkweed and prickles, most 'scruciating idle; and when anybody spoke to him he said "Humph!" Just "Humph!" and no more.

Presently the Horse came to him on Monday morning, with a saddle on his back and a bit in his mouth, and said, "Camel, O Camel, come out and trot like the rest of us."

"Humph!" said the Camel; and the Horse went away and told the Man.

Presently the Dog came to him, with a stick in his mouth, and said, "Camel, O Camel, come and fetch and carry like the rest of us."

"Humph!" said the Camel; and the Dog went away and told the Man.

# HOW THE CAMEL GOT HIS HUMP

Presently the Ox came to him, with the yoke on his neck, and said, "Camel, O Camel, come and plough like the rest of us."

"Humph!" said the Camel; and the Ox went away and told the Man.

At the end of the day the Man called the Horse and the Dog and the Ox together, and said, "Three, O Three, I'm very sorry for you (with the world so new-and-all); but that Humph-thing in the Desert can't work, or he would have been here by now, so I am going to leave him alone, and you must work double-time to make up for it."

That made the Three very angry (with the world so new-and-all), and they held a palaver, and an *indaba*, and a *punchayet*, and a pow-wow on the edge of the Desert; and the Camel came chewing milkweed *most* 'scruciating idle, and laughed at them. Then he said "Humph!" and went away again.

Presently there came along the Djinn in charge of All Deserts, rolling in a cloud of dust (Djinns always travel that way because it is Magic), and he stopped to palaver and pow-wow with the Three.

123

# HOW THE CAMEL GOT HIS HUMP

"Djinn of All Deserts," said the Horse, "*is* it right for any one to be idle, with the world so new-and-all?"

"Certainly not," said the Djinn.

"Well," said the Horse, "there's a thing in the middle of your Howling Desert (and he's a Howler himself) with a long neck and long legs, and he hasn't done a stroke of work since Monday morning. He won't trot."

"Whew!" said the Djinn, whistling, "that's my Camel, for all the gold in Arabia! What does he say about it?"

"He says 'Humph!'" said the Dog; "and he won't fetch and carry."

"Does he say anything else?"

"Only 'Humph!'; and he won't plough," said the Ox.

"Very good," said the Djinn. "I'll humph him if you will kindly wait a minute."

The Djinn rolled himself up in his dustcloak, and took a bearing across the desert, and found the Camel most 'scruciatingly idle, looking at his own reflection in a pool of water.

"My long and bubbling friend," said the Djinn, "what's this I hear of your doing no work, with the world so new-and all?"

"Humph!" said the Camel.

The Djinn sat down, with his chin in his hand, and began to think a Great Magic, while the Camel looked at his own reflection in the pool of water.

"You've given the Three extra work ever since Monday morning, all on account of your 'scruciating idleness," said the Djinn; and he went on thinking Magics, with his chin in his hand.

"Humph!" said the Camel.

"I shouldn't say that again if I were you," said the Djinn; "you might say it once too often. Bubbles, I want you to work."

And the Camel said "Humph!" again; but no sooner had he said it than he saw his back, that he was so proud of, puffing up and puffing up into a great big lolloping humph.

"Do you see that?" said the Djinn. "That's your very own humph that you've brought upon your very own self by not working. Today is Thursday, and you've done no work since Monday, when the work began. Now you are going to work."

"How can I," said the Camel, "with this humph on my back?"

"That's made a-purpose," said the Djinn, "all because you missed those three days. You will be able to work now for three days without eating, because you can live on your humph; and don't you ever say I never did anything for you. Come out of the Desert and go to the Three, and behave. Humph yourself!"

And the Camel humphed himself, humph and all, and went away to join the Three. And from that day to this the Camel always wears a humph (we call it 'hump' now, not to hurt his feelings); but he has never yet caught up with the three days that he missed at the beginning of the world, and he has never yet learned how to behave.

# ZOO CAKE

This is a classic Chocolate cake with vanilla frosting—but it's decorated with chocolate covered animal crackers! Add candles and this makes a great birthday cake for any animal lover.

GREAT
MEETING
*To be Held*
*in*
RESOLUTION
*to pass*
DEMANDING
MORE
FOOD

## CAKE BATTER:

6 tablespoons unsweetened cocoa powder

3 cups flour

2 cups sugar

2 teaspoons baking soda

1 teaspoon salt

¾ cup vegetable oil

3 tablespoons white vinegar

1 tablespoon vanilla extract

2 cups cold water

## FROSTING:

1 lb. box confectioner's sugar

8 tablespoons butter

1 tablespoon vanilla extract

3 tablespoons milk

## COOKIES:

¼ cup semisweet chocolate chips

1 ½ tablespoons butter

20 animal crackers

1. Preheat oven to 350° F.

2. To make cake batter, sift cocoa powder, flour, sugar, baking soda, and salt into one bowl.

3. Sift cocoa mixture back and forth between two bowls a total of three times.

4. Make three holes in the dry mix: one "Papa bear" size, one "Mama bear" size, and one "baby bear" size. Pour the vegetable oil into the large hole, pour the white vinegar into the medium hole, and pour the vanilla extract into the baby hole.

5. Add cold water and whisk together quickly.

6. Divide batter between two 8 ½-inch round cake pans and pop into oven with minimum delay. Bake for approximately 40 minutes or until an inserted toothpick comes out clean. Place on a cake rack to cool.

7. To make chocolate animal crackers, melt chocolate chips and butter together on top of a double boiler and stir well.

8. When chocolate is completely melted, remove from heat. Drop crackers into warm chocolate mixture, one at a time. Remove with a fork, letting extra chocolate drip off, and lay on a piece of waxed paper to harden.

9. To prepare vanilla frosting, heat butter in the microwave on medium heat for approximately 20 to 30 seconds or until soft.

10. In a large mixing bowl, combine sugar, butter, vanilla and milk and beat until completely blended and smooth.

11. Smooth frosting onto the top of one half of your cake, and then place the other half on top. Ice top and sides with remaining frosting.

12. Press chocolate animal crackers into the frosting along the sides of the cake and stand them upright on top of the cake!

*Serves eight*

# TIGER IN THE JUNGLE

*AUTHOR UNKNOWN*

Last night I dreamt I was a
   tiger in the jungle,
A great BIG tiger!
'Til a lion ate me
Then there wasn't anything
   I couldn't do,
'Til they caught me
   and they brought me
   to the zoo.
Then I was a dancing bear,
I danced bare,
'Cause that's how dancing
   bears dance.
But I was sneezing,
   and I was freezing,

Because I was a dancing
   polar bear.
Then I was a crocodile,
No an alligator,
No a crocodile,
With four funny little legs
   that were
   no good for dancing!
Then I woke up,
And I was me,
Just me.
I enjoy being an…OYSTER!

# ANIMAL PUPPETS

**C**hildren, children everywhere, with animals on their arms.
Just what is that child doing, looking like a walking farm?
Frogs, ducks, hogs and dogs—the possibilities are endless!
Make enough animal puppets and you will never be friendless.
Glitter, googly eyes, and pipe cleaners, too—
Add what you want until you have your own zoo.

# Paper Bag Puppets

paper bag, construction paper, crayons, glue, scissors

*optional*: tissue paper, glitter, yarn, pipe cleaners

1. Get your hands on a brown paper lunch bag and think of an animal. The flat bottom of the bag will become your animal's face. You can also extend the length of the face by attaching a piece of construction paper to make the long jaws of an alligator or the beak of a bird.

2. Draw the animal's face directly onto the bag or cut out its features from construction paper and paste on the eyes, ears, and nose. You might want to add some other details, like a long strip of red paper for a snake or frog's tongue or glitter for a fish's scales. Yarn or fringed paper makes great fur, and you can use pipe cleaners as whiskers.

3. Glue on the hands, feet or paws, and any other features of your puppet. If it's a bug, for example, tissue paper wings and a pair of antennae might be necessary. Use crayons to add special markings like spots, stripes, scales, or fur. Glue on a tail, and you're ready to go. Make two—one for each arm—and your animal puppets can talk to each other.

# Mouth Puppets

crayons, 8 ½" x 11" sheet of paper, glue

1.  Fold the sheet of paper into three equal sections, lengthwise.

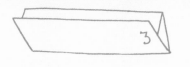

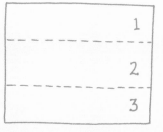

2.  Then fold it in half width-wise, to make a tent.

3.  Fold each half of the tent in half again to create a *W* shape.

4. Draw an animal face on the outside and a mouth on the inside. Tuck your hand into the openings, and chatter away!

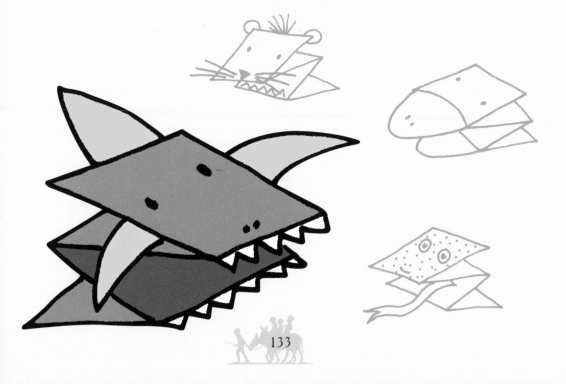

# LILY AND THE LION

Once upon a time, there was a merchant who had three lovely daughters. As he prepared to go away for a long trip, he asked each daughter what present she would like him to bring home. His oldest daughter longed for shiny pearls; the middle daughter wished for sparkling gems; and his youngest, named Lily, asked only for a single red rose. The merchant knew that finding a rose in winter would be nearly impossible, but he promised to do his best.

On his travels, the merchant met a jeweler who sold him pearls and gems. But, though he searched high and low, he could not find a red rose. He asked the townspeople, and they all laughed. "Don't you know, roses don't grow in the snow!" Finally, he came to a castle that was surrounded by an enchanted garden. Half of the garden was hidden under the snow, but the other half was as glorious as in summertime. "What luck!" cried the merchant. He entered the garden and plucked the loveliest rose for his little Lily.

Suddenly, a fierce lion appeared. "How dare you steal from my garden?" he snarled. "I will eat you alive!"

# LILY AND THE LION

"B-b-b-b-but, Mr. Lion, it was an honest mistake," stuttered the merchant. "P-p-p-p-please let me go! I'll give you anything you want!"

"Very well," roared the lion. "You will give me the first thing you see upon returning home. Only then will I let you keep your life and my rose."

The merchant was terrified. Lily was always the first to greet him at the door. But he feared that if he didn't agree to the lion's demands, he would not escape alive. He had to take the chance.

But no sooner had the merchant reached his front path than Lily burst out of the house and leaped into his arms. "Oh, Papa, you found my rose," she cried with glee. But the merchant did not share his daughter's joy.

He told her of the high price he would have to pay for the rose, and begged her to hide quickly.

But Lily was not afraid. "Tomorrow I will visit the lion," she said. "I will calm him, and he will let me go." So the next morning, Lily set off in search of the lion. As evening neared, she arrived at the castle gates. But instead of the fierce lion, Lily found an enchanted prince! He welcomed her warmly and explained that he and his courtiers lived as lions by day, but that they were turned back to their human forms after sundown. Lily was so touched by the prince's kindness that she agreed to marry him. They lived very happily together.

Nearly a year had passed when the prince learned that his bride's oldest sister was to be married. Lily decided to make a surprise appearance at the wedding and traveled the long distance home alone. Lily's family was shocked and amazed to see her, for they had assumed that the lion had gobbled her up. After the joyous ceremony and feast, Lily returned to her prince.

Before long, the prince announced that Lily's middle sister was to be married. Lily asked her husband to join her on this trip, but he refused. "If any torchlight touches me," said the prince, "I will be turned into a dove and forced to fly the earth for seven years." But Lily pleaded with him until he finally agreed to go. When they arrived at the wedding, Lily led the prince to a large enclosed hall. She promised that the thick walls would protect him from the

light. Unhappily, no one had noticed a crack in the door. So when the wedding party passed from the church, a ray of torchlight fell upon the prince.

When Lily came to escort the prince to the marriage feast, he was gone. In his place she found a dove. "For seven years I will fly the earth," said the white bird. "Now and then a feather will fall so you can follow my path." And with that, the dove took flight.

Lily followed the dove for many long years. When the seventh year was over, she rejoiced. But sadly, she didn't see the last feather drop, and so lost track of her true love. Heartbroken, Lily called up to the sun and asked, "Great light that warms my skin, have you seen my dear dove?"

# LILY AND THE LION

"No," said the sun. "Take this treasure chest. Open it when you need it most."

Lily then asked the moon, "Pale glow that chases me, have you seen my dear dove?"

"No," said the moon. "Take this egg. Break it when you need it most."

Lily then asked the north wind, "Cold wind that makes me shiver, have you seen my dear dove?"

"No," said the north wind. "I will ask the other winds. Perhaps they have seen it." But neither the east or west winds had seen the dove.

Then the south wind came and said, "I have seen your white dove. He has since turned back into a lion, and is at the edge of the Red Sea, fighting a dragon. But it is no ordinary dragon; it is an enchanted princess who wishes to separate you and your lion."

Then the north wind said, "Go to the Red Sea. Find the rods that stand on the north shore. Count to the eleventh rod and break it off. Use it to slay the dragon. Your lion will regain his human form. Quickly take him aboard the griffin (the eagle-winged lion) that waits by the Red Sea. The griffin will carry you home. Here is a nut. Once you are halfway across the sea, drop it down to the water. A great tree will rise up for the griffin to rest on. Otherwise, the griffin will not be able to get you across, and he will toss you into the sea."

Lily thanked the winds and traveled to the Red Sea. She found the rods just as the north wind described them. She counted to the eleventh rod, broke it off,

and speared the dragon. The prince regained his human form, and the dragon turned into the enchanted princess. Lily ran toward her prince, but before she could reach him, the princess grabbed hold of him and cast an evil spell over him. To Lily's horror, they mounted the griffin and flew away.

Lily pledged to find her prince. She traveled through the desert until she came to a great castle where the prince and princess were to be married that evening. Lily opened the treasure chest. Inside she found a dress of gold as bright as the sun. She put it on and entered the castle. When the princess saw the golden gown, she wanted it for herself. "Neither silver nor gold can buy this gown," said Lily. "I will accept nothing less than flesh and blood."

The princess did not understand. Lily explained that she wanted the wedding to be postponed and to have a moment alone with the prince. That night, the princess ordered one of her servants to deliver a sleeping potion to the prince. When Lily came to his room, he was already numb with sleep. She spoke to her prince while he slept. "I have followed you for seven long years. The sun, the moon, and the four winds have brought us together again. Please know that I still love you, and will never give up hope." Lily's voice blew by the prince like a whispering breeze, but he did not hear her words.

As Lily was escorted out of the castle, she vowed to keep trying to save her prince. Alone, beneath the night sky, Lily pulled from her pocket the egg given to her by the moon and cracked it open. Out popped a golden hen and six golden chicks. Sparkling in the moonlight, they looked like beautiful dancing jewels.

The next morning, Lily brought them to the princess, and the princess wanted them for herself. "Neither silver nor gold can buy these fowl," said Lily. "I will except nothing less than flesh and blood." Lily again requested a moment alone with the prince in his bedchamber. That night, the princess ordered the servant to deliver the same sleeping potion to the prince. But the servant, who had witnessed Lily's visit the night before, was so moved by her plight that he told the prince everything he'd seen and threw away the potion.

Lily came again, after the prince had fallen asleep. She said, "I have followed you for seven long years. The sun, the moon, and the four winds have brought us together again...." Suddenly the prince awoke, as from a dream. Lily's voice had broken the princess's spell.

With the servant's help, Lily and the prince crept out of the castle and traveled to the Red Sea. There they found the griffin waiting for them. They climbed on his back and he carried them up into the sky. Lily dropped the nut halfway across the sea, and a great tree sprang up. After the griffin was rested, they continued on until they were home. Lily and the prince lived happily ever after.

A leopard cannot

change its spots

# WILD ANIMAL FACTS

✳ Unlike other reptiles, crocodiles have ears and nostrils that
seal up when they dive. They also have a third, semitransparent
eyelid they use like goggles to see underwater.

✳ Elephants can't jump!

✳ The giraffe is the tallest of all animals, standing as hig

✳ Koalas don't have sweat glands, so they cool off by
licking their arms and stretching out in the trees.

✳ Orangutans have been known to make masks of small
branches to protect their faces when raiding honeybee nests.

✳ The adult hedgehog has up to 5,000 spines covering its body
and can roll into a prickly ball when threatened!

＊ When a zebra mates with a donkey, its offspring is called a "zebdonk"!

＊ Snow leopards use their 3-foot-long tails as mufflers to protect their noses and lungs from the cold at night.

as 18 feet. Giraffe calves are usually 6 feet tall at birth.

＊ Spotted hyenas have the most powerful jaws in the animal kingdom. They can crush even the largest bones as if they were twigs—and then eat and digest them along with the horns and teeth of their prey.

＊ There's only a 1% difference between chimp DNA and human DNA.

＊ Who needs a cup? When a gorilla is thirsty she soaks her fur in water and then sucks the water off.

# Animal Jokes

What horse is never seen
in the daytime?
*A nightmare.*

What do you give a sick bird?
*Tweetment.*

What is the best year
for a kangaroo?
*Leap year.*

What did the boy octopus say
to the girl octopus?
*I want to hold your hand, hand, hand,
hand, hand, hand, hand, hand.*

Why do hummingbirds hum?
*Because they don't know the words.*

Why are elephants poor?
*Because they work for peanuts.*

How do fleas travel from
place to place?
*By itch hiking.*

What bird never goes to a barber?
*A bald eagle.*

What time is it when an elephant
sits on your bed?
*Time to get a new bed.*

What happens when you tell a
duck a joke?
*It quacks up.*

How do you fix a broken gorilla?
*With a monkey wrench.*

What is the best way to catch
a squirrel?
*Climb up a tree and act like a nut.*

# Bird Sayings

*And what they mean*

## The chickens come home to roost

*You always have to face the consequences of your actions.*

## Don't count your chickens before they hatch

*Don't rely on anything
until it actually happens.*

## Like water off a duck's back

*Rolls off easily; no big deal.*

## Eat crow

*Take back your words.*

## If it walks like a duck, quacks like a duck, and looks like a duck, it must be a duck

*If something acts, sounds, and appears to be true, it probably is.*

# SWALLOWS

## BY REBECCA McCANN

I love to watch the swallows soar.

With lilting rhythmic grace they fly,

As if a flock of small black notes

Were writing music on the sky.

# THE HAPPY PRINCE

### BY OSCAR WILDE

High above the city, on a tall column, stood the statue of the Happy Prince. He was gilded all over with thin leaves of fine gold, for eyes he had two bright sapphires, and a large red ruby glowed on his sword hilt.

He was very much admired indeed. "He is as beautiful as a weathercock," remarked one of the Town Councillors who wished to gain a reputation for having artistic tastes; "only not quite so useful," he added, fearing lest people should think him unpractical, which he really was not.

"Why can't you be like the Happy Prince?" asked a sensible mother of her little boy who was crying for the moon. "The Happy Prince never dreams of crying for anything."

"I am glad there is someone in the world who is quite happy," muttered a disappointed man as he gazed at the wonderful statue.

"He looks just like an angel," said the Charity Children as they came out of the cathedral in their bright scarlet cloaks and their clean white pinafores.

"How do you know?" said the Mathematical Master, "you have never seen one."

# THE HAPPY PRINCE

"Ah! but we have, in our dreams," answered the children; and the Mathematical Master frowned and looked very severe, for he did not approve of children dreaming.

One night there flew over the city a little Swallow. His friends had gone away to Egypt six weeks before, but he had stayed behind, for he was in love with the most beautiful Reed.

"It is a ridiculous attachment," twittered the other Swallows, "she has no money, and far too many relations"; and indeed the river was quite full of Reeds.

After they had gone he felt lonely, and began to tire of his ladylove. "She has no conversation," he said, "and I am afraid that she is a coquette, for she is always flirting with the wind." And certainly, whenever the wind blew, the Reed made the most graceful curtsies.

"Will you come away with me?" he said finally to her; but the Reed shook her head, she was so attached to her home.

"You have been trifling with me," he cried. "I am off to the Pyramids. Good-bye!" and he flew away.

# THE HAPPY PRINCE

All day long he flew, and at nighttime he arrived at the city. "Where shall I put up?" he said; "I hope the town has made preparations."

Then he saw the statue on the tall column.

"I will put up there," he cried; "it is a fine position, with plenty of fresh air." So he alighted just between the feet of the Happy Prince.

"I have a golden bedroom," he said softly to himself as he looked around, and he prepared to go to sleep; but just as he was putting his head under his wing a large drop of water fell on him.

"What is the use of a statue if it cannot keep the rain off?" he said; "I must look for a good chimney pot," and he determined to fly away.

But before he had opened his wings, a third drop fell, and he looked up, and saw—Ah! what did he see?

The eyes of the Happy Prince were filled with tears, and tears were running down his golden cheeks. His face was so beautiful in the moonlight that the little Swallow was filled with pity.

"Who are you?" he said.

"I am the Happy Prince."

"Why are you weeping then?" asked the Swallow; "you have quite drenched me."

"When I was alive and had a human heart," answered the statue, "I did not know what tears were, for I lived in the Palace of Sans-Souci, where sorrow is not allowed to enter. In the daytime I played with my companions in the garden, and in the evening I led

# THE HAPPY PRINCE

the dance in the Great Hall. Around the garden ran a very lofty wall, but I never cared to ask what lay beyond it, everything around me was so beautiful. My courtiers called me the Happy Prince, and happy indeed I was, if pleasure be happiness. So I lived, and so I died. And now that I am dead they have set me up here so high that I can see all the ugliness and all the misery of my city, and though my heart is made of lead yet I cannot choose but weep."

"What! Is he not solid gold?" said the Swallow to himself. He was too polite to make any personal remarks out loud.

"Far away," continued the statue in a low musical voice, "far away in a little street there is a poor house. One of the windows is open, and through it I can see a woman seated at a table. Her face is thin and worn, and she has coarse, red hands, all pricked by the needle, for she is a seamstress. In a bed in the corner of the room her little boy

# THE HAPPY PRINCE

is lying ill. He has a fever, and is asking for oranges. His mother has nothing to give him but river water, so he is crying. Swallow, Swallow, little Swallow, will you not bring her the ruby out of my sword-hilt? My feet are fastened to this pedestal and I cannot move."

"I am waited for in Egypt," said the Swallow.

"Swallow, Swallow, little Swallow," said the Prince, "will you not stay with me for one night, and be my messenger? The boy is so thirsty, and the mother so sad."

The Happy Prince looked so sad that the little Swallow was sorry. "It is very cold here," he said; "but I will stay with you for one night, and be your messenger."

"Thank you, little Swallow," said the Prince.

So the Swallow picked out the great ruby from the Prince's sword, and flew away with it in his beak over the roofs of the town. At last he came to the poor house and looked in. The boy was tossing feverishly on his bed, and the mother had fallen asleep, she was so tired. In he hopped, and laid the great ruby on the table beside the woman's thimble. Then he flew gently round the bed, fanning the boy's forehead with his wings. "How cool I feel," said the boy, "I must be getting better;" and he sank into a delicious slumber.

Then the Swallow flew back to the Happy Prince, and told him what he had done. "It is curious," he

remarked, "but I feel quite warm now, although it is so cold."

"That is because you have done a good action," said the Prince. And the little swallow began to think, and then he fell asleep. Thinking always made him sleepy.

When day broke he flew down to the river and had a bath. "What a remarkable phenomenon," said the Professor of Ornithology as he was passing over the bridge. "A swallow in winter!" And he wrote a long letter about it to the local newspaper. Everyone quoted it, it was full of so many words that they could not understand.

"Tonight I go to Egypt," said the Swallow, and he was in high spirits at the prospect.

When the moon rose he flew back to the Happy Prince. "Have you any commissions for Egypt?" he cried; "I am just starting."

"Swallow, Swallow, little Swallow," said the Prince, "will you not stay with me one night longer?"

"It is winter," answered the Swallow, "and the chill snow will soon be here. In Egypt the sun is warm on the green palm trees, and the crocodiles lie in the mud and look lazily about them. Dear Prince, I must leave you, but I will never forget you"

"In the square below," said the Happy Prince, "there stands a little matchgirl. She has let her matches fall in the gutter, and they are all spoiled. She has no shoes or stockings, and her little head is bare. Pluck out my eye and give it to her."

"I will stay with you one night longer," said the Swallow, "but I cannot pluck out your eye. You would be quite blind then."

"Swallow, Swallow, little Swallow," said the Prince, "do as I command you."

So he plucked out the Prince's eye, and darted down with it. He swooped past the matchgirl, and slipped the jewel into the palm of her hand. "What a lovely bit of glass," cried the little girl; and she ran home, laughing.

Then the Swallow came back to the Prince. "You are blind now," he said, "so I will stay with you always."

"No, little Swallow," said the poor Prince, "you must go away to Egypt."

"I will stay with you always," said the Swallow, and he slept at the Prince's feet.

All the next day he sat on the Prince's shoulder, and told him stories of what he had seen in strange lands.

"Dear little Swallow," said the Prince, "you tell me of marvelous things, but more marvelous than anything is the suffering of men and of women. There is no Mystery so great as Misery. Fly over my city, little Swallow, and tell me what you see there."

So the Swallow flew over the great city, and saw the rich making merry in their beautiful houses, while the beggars were sitting at the gates. He flew into dark lanes, and saw the white faces of starving children looking out listlessly at the black streets. Under the archway of a bridge two little boys were lying in one another's arms to try and keep themselves warm. "How hungry we are!" they said. "You must not lie here," shouted the Watchman, and they wandered out into the rain.

Then he flew back and told the Prince what he had seen.

"I am covered with fine gold," said the Prince, "you must take it off, leaf by leaf, and give it to my poor; the living always think that gold can make them happy."

Leaf after leaf of the fine gold the Swallow picked off, till the Happy Prince looked quite dull and gray. Leaf after leaf of the fine gold he brought to the poor, and the children's faces grew rosier, and they laughed and played games in the street. "We have bread now!" they cried.

Then the snow came, and after the snow came the frost. The streets looked as if they were made of silver, they were so bright and glistening; long icicles like crystal daggers hung down from the eaves of the houses, everybody went about in furs, and the little boys wore scarlet caps and skated on the ice.

The poor little Swallow grew colder and colder, but he would not leave the Prince, he loved him too well. He picked up crumbs outside the baker's door when the baker was not looking, and tried to keep himself warm by flapping his wings.

But at last he knew that he was going to die. He had just strength to fly up to the Prince's shoulder once more. "Goodbye, dear Prince!" he murmured, "will you let me kiss your hand?"

"I am glad that you are going to Egypt at last, little Swallow," said the Prince, "you have stayed too long here; but you must kiss me on the lips, for I love you."

"It is not to Egypt that I am going," said the Swallow. "I am going to the House of Death. Death is the brother of Sleep, is he not?"

And he kissed the Happy Prince on the lips, and fell down dead at his feet.

At that moment a curious crack sounded inside the statue, as if something had broken. The fact is that the leaden heart had snapped right in two. It certainly was a dreadfully hard frost.

Early the next morning the Mayor was walking in the square below in company with the Town Councillors. As they passed the column he looked up at the statue: "Dear me! how shabby the Happy Prince looks!" he said.

"How shabby indeed!" cried the Town Councillors, who always agreed with the Mayor; and they went up to look at it.

"The ruby has fallen out of his sword, his eyes are gone, and he is golden no longer," said the Mayor; "in fact, he is little better than a beggar!"

"Little better than a beggar," said the Town Councillors.

"And here is actually a dead bird at his feet!" continued the Mayor. "We must really issue a proclamation that birds are not to be allowed to die here." And the Town Clerk made a note of the suggestion.

So they pulled down the statue of the Happy Prince. "As he is no longer beautiful he is no longer useful," said the Art Professor at the University.

Then they melted the statue in a furnace, and the Mayor held a meeting of the Corporation to decide what was to be done with the metal. "We must have another statue, of course," he said, "and it shall be a statue of myself."

"Of myself," said each of the Town Councillors, and they quarreled. When I last heard of them they were quarreling still.

"What a strange thing!" said the overseer of the workmen at the foundry. "This broken lead heart will not melt in the furnace. We must throw it away." So they threw in on a dustheap where the dead Swallow was also lying.

"Bring me the two most precious things in the city," said God to one of His Angels; and the Angel brought Him the leaden heart and the dead bird.

"You have rightly chosen," said God, "for in my garden of Paradise this little bird shall sing for evermore, and in my city of gold the Happy Prince shall praise me."

# FOR THE BIRDS

As spring approaches each year, the birds return from their tropical winter getaways down south in search of more moderate climates. What better way to welcome back our feathered friends than to offer them a place to feed and wash themselves after their long journey? Feeders and baths are also a fun way to observe the birds in your area and identify different species. Try these simple ideas when the flock starts to settle back in.

## Bagel Bird Feeder

*day-old bagel, lard or peanut butter, birdseed, string*

1. Here's a very basic feeder that the birds will love. Take a day-old bagel and spread lard or peanut butter all over the it.

2. Put the bagel into a plastic bag, add birdseed, and shake until the bagel is evenly coated with seed.

3. Loop a string through the bagel's hole and hang it on a tree. The best thing about this feeder is that the birds will keep eating it until it's all gone!

# Terra-cotta Birdbath

terra-cotta pot, glazed saucer, acrylic paints, brush,
water-based polyurethane, silicone glue

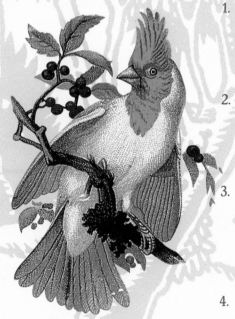

1. Flip the pot over and use the paints to decorate the outside any way you like. (Do not paint the glazed saucer.) Allow the paint to dry.

2. Go over the outside of the newly painted pot with three coats of polyurethane to protect the paint and help keep the water from seeping into the clay.

3. After letting the polyurethane sealant dry, use the silicone glue to secure the bottom of the pot to the bottom of the glazed saucer. The pot should look like a stand for the birdbath now.

4. Fill the birdbath with water, place it outdoors, and make sure there are no hungry cats around!

Birds of a feather

flock together

# INCHWORM

Two and two are four, four and four

Inch - worm, inch - worm, mea - sur - ing the

are eight, Eight and eight are six - teen,

ma - ri - golds. You and your a - rith - ma - tic, you'll

six - teen and six - teen are thir - ty - two,

prob - a - bly go far. _____

2. Inch worm, Inchworm, measuring the marigolds,
seems to me you'd stop and see how beautiful they are.

# BIRD FACTS

✳ Male bowerbirds build arched, hutlike structures called bowers
out of twigs and decorate them with various colorful objects
such as feathers, shells, and flowers in order to attract a mate.
Using a piece of bark as a brush, satin bowerbirds will even
paint their bowers with fruit pulp!

✳ With a diving speed of well over 100 mph,
the peregrine falcon is the fastest bird.

✳ Though penguins can't fly, they can jump as high as 6 feet in the air.

✳ The brain of an ostrich is only as large a

✳ The only bird that can fly backwards is the hummingbird.

✳ An eagle can look straight ahead and down at the ground at
the same time with the same eye. Now you know where the
expression "eagle-eyed" comes from.

✳ All birds can turn their heads 360 degrees. Now that's flexibility!

✳ Some birds would rather use ants than soap—to clean their feathers, that is. The birds will pick up live ants and twist and turn to stroke their feathers with them.

✳ The eagle has a third transparent eyelid that acts like a pair of built-in sunglasses, allowing the bird to look directly at the sun.

✳ Oxpeckers make a meal of insects that live in the hair of oxen and other large African mammals. This arrangement benefits both the oxpecker, who has a constant supply of food, and the host animal, who is cleaned of insects that may carry disease.

its eye—but its egg is bigger than its brain!

✳ Some birds go fishing just like humans do! Green herons drop live insects, berries, or other flashy items from the air onto the surface of the water to lure fish. When a fish takes the bait, the heron goes for it!

✳ Cranes navigate long distances using the stars and planets, just as human pilots used to do before radar was invented.

# CHICKEN LITTLE

Once upon a time, there was a tiny chicken named Chicken Little. One day, Chicken Little was walking through the woods when, all of a sudden, an acorn fell and hit her on the head—*KERPLUNK!*

"Goodness gracious!" said Chicken Little. "The sky is falling! I must warn the king."

On her way to see the king, Chicken Little met up with Henny Penny, who said, "I'm going to the woods to hunt for worms."

"Oh, no! You can't go!" said Chicken Little. "The sky is falling! Come with me to tell the king."

So they went along and went along as fast as they could.

Soon they met Cocky Locky, who said, "I'm going to the woods to find some seeds."

"Oh, no! You can't go!" said Henny Penny. "The sky is falling! Come with us to tell the king."

So they went along and went along as fast as they could.

Soon they met Goosey Loosey, who said, "I'm going to the woods to look for berries."

"Oh, no! You can't go!" said Cocky Locky. "The sky is falling! Come with us to tell the king."

# CHICKEN LITTLE

So they went along and went along as fast as they could.

Soon they met up with wily old Foxy Woxy.

"Where are you going, my fine feathered friends?" asked Foxy Woxy. He spoke softly, so as not to frighten them.

"The sky is falling!" cried Chicken Little. "We must tell the king."

"I know a secret shortcut," said Foxy Woxy. "Follow me."

But wicked Foxy Woxy did not lead the others to the king's palace. He led them straight to his foxhole, where he planned to gobble them up.

Just as Chicken Little and the others were about to go in, they heard a loud ruckus and stopped. It was the king's hunting dogs, growling and howling. They chased Foxy Woxy across the meadow and through the woods. They chased him far, far away and he never came back.

After that day, Chicken Little always carried an umbrella when she walked in the woods. The umbrella was a present from the king. Whenever an acorn fell— *KERPLUNK!*—Chicken Little didn't even flinch. In fact, she didn't notice it at all.

# THE THREE FOXES

BY A. A. MILNE

Once upon a time there were three little foxes
Who didn't wear stockings, and they didn't wear sockses,
But they all had handkerchiefs to blow their noses,
And they kept their handkerchiefs in cardboard boxes.

They lived in the forest in three little houses,
And they didn't wear coats, and they didn't wear trousies.
They ran through the woods on their little bare tootsies,
And they played 'Touch last' with a family of mouses.

They didn't go shopping in the High Street shopses,
But caught what they wanted in the woods and copses.
They all went fishing, and they caught three wormses,
They went out hunting, and they caught three wopses.

They went to a Fair, and they all won prizes—
Three plum-puddingses and three mince-pieses.
They rode on elephants and swang on swingses,
And hit three coco-nuts at coco-nut shieses.

That's all that I know of the three little foxes
Who kept their handkerchiefs in cardboard boxes.
They lived in the forest in three little houses,
But they didn't wear coats and they didn't wear trousies,
And they didn't wear stockings and they didn't wear sockses.

# Animal Riddles

1. What is as big as an elephant, but weighs nothing?

2. I have a little house in which I live all alone. It has no doors or windows, and if I want to go out I must break through the wall. What am I?

3. A farmer needs to get a fox, a chicken, and a bag of grain across a river. He has a boat, but can only take one item at a time. The fox will eat the chicken if they are left alone. The chicken will eat the grain if they are left alone. How can he do it?

4. If a rooster laid a brown egg and a white egg, what kind of chicks would hatch?

5. How many animals of each species did Moses take with him on the Ark?

6. A farmer had seventeen sheep. All but nine died. How many does he have left?

**Answers:** 1. His shadow. 2. A chicken in an egg. 3. First he takes the chicken across. Then he takes the bag of grain across. Then he takes the fox across. Finally he goes back for the chicken and takes him across. 4. None. Roosters don't lay eggs. 5. None; Moses wasn't on the Ark, Noah was. 6. Nine

177

# THE LITTLE PRINCE

BY *Antoine de Saint-Exupéry*

It was then that the fox appeared.

"Good morning," said the fox.

"Good morning," the little prince answered politely, though when he turned around he saw nothing.

"Who are you?" the little prince asked. "You're very pretty..."

"I'm a fox," the fox said.

"Come and play with me," the little prince proposed. "I'm feeling so sad."

"I can't play with you," the fox said. "I'm not tamed."

"Ah! Excuse me," said the little prince. But upon reflection he added, "What does *tamed* mean?"

"You're not from around here," the fox said. "What are you looking for?"

"I'm looking for people," said the little prince. "What does *tamed* mean?"

"People," said the fox, "have guns and they hunt. It's quite troublesome. And they also raise chickens. That's the only interesting thing about them. Are you looking for chickens?"

"No," said the little prince, "I'm looking for friends. What does *tamed* mean?"

"It's something that's been too often neglected. It means, 'to create ties'..."

"'To create ties'?"

"That's right," the fox said. "For me you're only a little boy just like a hundred thousand other little boys. And I have no need of you. And you have no need of me, either. For you I'm only a fox like a hundred thousand other foxes. But if you tame me, we'll need each other. You'll be the only boy in the world for me. I'll be the only fox in the world for you . . ."

"I'm beginning to understand," the little prince said. "There's a flower . . . I think she's tamed me . . ."

"Possibly," the fox said. "On Earth, one sees all kinds of things."

"Oh, this isn't on Earth," the little prince said.

The fox seemed quite intrigued. "On another planet?"

"Yes."

"Are there hunters on that planet?"

"No."

"Now that's interesting. And chickens?"

"No."

"Nothing's perfect," sighed the fox.

But he returned to his idea. "My life is monotonous. I hunt chickens; people hunt me. All chickens are just alike, and all men are just alike. So I'm rather bored. But if you tame me, my life will be filled with sunshine. I'll know the sound of footsteps that will be different from all the rest. Other footsteps send me back underground. Yours will call me out of my burrow like music. And then, look! You see the wheat fields over there? I don't eat bread. For me wheat is of no use whatever. Wheat fields say nothing to me. Which is sad. But you have hair the color of gold. So it will be wonderful, once you've tamed me! The wheat,

180

which is golden, will remind me of you. And I'll love the sound of the wind in the wheat..."

The fox fell silent and stared at the little prince for a long while. "Please... tame me!" he said.

"I'd like to," the little prince replied, "but I haven't much time. I have friends to find and so many things to learn."

"The only things you learn are the things you tame," said the fox. "People haven't time to learn anything. They buy things ready-made in stores. But since there are no stores where you can buy friends, people no longer have friends. If you want a friend, tame me!"

"What do I have to do?" asked the little prince.

"You have to be very patient," the fox answered. "First you'll sit down a little ways away from me, over there,

in the grass. I'll watch you out of the corner of my eye, and you won't say anything. Language is the source of misunderstandings. But day by day, you'll be able to sit a little closer..."

The next day the little prince returned.

"It would have been better to return at the same time," the fox said. "For instance, if you come at four in the afternoon, I'll begin to be happy by three. The closer it gets to four, the happier I'll feel. By four I'll be all excited and worried; I'll discover what it costs to be happy! But if you come at any old time, I'll never know when I should prepare my heart.... There must be rites."

"What's a *rite*?" asked the little prince.

"That's another thing that's been too often neglected," said the fox.

# THE LITTLE PRINCE

"It's the fact that one day is different from the other days, one hour from the other hours. My hunters, for example, have a rite. They dance with the village girls on Thursdays. So Thursday's a wonderful day: I can take a stroll all the way to the vineyards. If the hunters danced whenever they chose, the days would all be just alike, and I'd have no holiday at all."

That was how the little prince tamed the fox. And when the time to leave was near:

"Ah!" the fox said. "I shall weep."

"It's your own fault," the little prince said. "I never wanted to do you any harm, but you insisted that I tame you . . ."

"Yes, of course," the fox said.

"But you're going to weep!" said the little prince.

"Yes, of course," the fox said.

"Then you get nothing out of it?"

"I get something," the fox said, "because of the color of the wheat." Then he added, "Go look at the roses again. You'll understand that yours is the only rose in all the world. Then come back to say good-bye, and I'll make you the gift of a secret."

The little prince went to look at the roses again.

"You're not at all like my rose. You're nothing at all yet," he told them. "No one has tamed you and you haven't tamed anyone. You're the way my fox was. He was just a fox like a hundred thousand others. But I've made him my friend, and now he's the only fox in all the world."

And the roses were humbled.

"You're lovely, but you're empty," he went on. "One couldn't die for you. Of course, an ordinary passerby would think my rose looked just like you. But my rose, all on her own, is more important than all of you together, since she's the one I've watered. Since she's the one I put under glass. Since she's the one I sheltered behind a screen. Since she's the one for whom I killed the caterpillars (except the two or three for butterflies). Since she's the one I listened to when she complained, or when she boasted, or even sometimes when she said nothing at all. Since she's *my* rose."

And he went back to the fox. "Good-bye," he said.

"Good-bye," said the fox. "Here is my secret. It's quite simple: One sees clearly only with the heart. Anything essential is invisible to the eyes."

"Anything essential is invisible to the eyes," the little prince repeated, in order to remember.

"It's the time you spent on your rose that makes your rose so important."

"It's the time I spent on my rose...," the little prince repeated, in order to remember.

"People have forgotten this truth," the fox said. "But you mustn't forget it. You become responsible forever for what you've tamed. You're responsible for your rose..."

"I'm responsible for my rose...," the little prince repeated, in order to remember.

# SHADOW PUPPETS

## hands, light, a wall

**W**ould you believe that there are animals that can only be seen in the dark? To glimpse them, all you need is a lamp, a bare wall, your hands, and a good pair of sharp owl eyes. Before you know it, little critters will be jumping out from the shadows right in front of you.

Twitch your rabbit's ears by moving the third and fourth fingers of your left hand.

Pull your right thumb away from your fingers to make a panther roar.

Wiggle your fingers to make the spider walk.

Move your right thumb
for a boxing wallaby.

Wave your hands to
make the bird fly.

Try moving your hands so
that your dog sniffs the air.

*paper plate*

Shift your fourth finger
and pinky to make the
birds talk.

Pull back your right
arm to make the snail
disappear into its shell.

# THE PANTHER

### BY OGDEN NASH

The panther is like a leopard,
Except it hasn't been peppered.
Should you behold a panther crouch,
Prepare to say Ouch.
Better yet, if called by a panther,
Don't anther.

# SCARLETT SAVES HER FAMILY

### BY JANE MARTIN AND J. C. SUARÈS

The firemen at Hook & Ladder Company 175, 165 Bradford Street, were just wrapping up a long night's worth of calls, little fires mostly, people calling them for everything, including water leaks. They had three hours left until the tour was over. Maybe nothing would come in. But, as always, the bell rang. Four bells—which meant, "Your rest is over guys, get on the truck." From the dispatch they knew a few things right away. It was not the first fire for this building, an abandoned garage on Livonia, south of Barbey. And, though the place was frequently inhabited by street people, the firemen would not be allowed to go inside to find them. The garage was what firemen call bad; the parapet had a gaping crack and leaned far out, threatening to crash down to the sidewalk, and the inside beams were unstable. After a fireman had been killed in a recent building collapse, the NYFD had changed its SOP—standard operating procedures. This fire would be fought at a distance. Theirs would be an outside attack.

Snow driving around them, they pulled onto Barbey Street with Fireman Giannelli at the wheel, swinging wide at the corners to make the rear driver's job easier, going as fast as he could without running stop signs and red lights. And as the dispatcher buzzed confirmations from the first-due company on the scene that yes, this was a biggie, everyone on the truck saw the thick black column punching into the dawn sky—that column of hot smoke—and their adrenaline rushed.

As they pulled up, they took a look at the fire. It filled the dilapidated garage, which was flanked on one side by an abandoned two-story brick house, then by two wood-framed houses, one full of tenants. Two companies were already on the scene, starting to stretch a hose line. The street was filled with trucks when the guys jumped off with the lieutenant, all in full gear: turnout coat, mask, gloves, bunker pants; axes and halligans, sledge-hammers and hooks. Dave Giannelli looked for a parking space. With the engine truck on one side, another engine on the hydrant next to him, another hook-and-ladder, and the chief's Suburban, he didn't want to block the street. He pulled over and grabbed his coat and mask.

The fire had probably been going a while, at least two or three minutes, and it was no self-starter. It raged out of the open garage in an angry mass of flame and spark, blazing with the health—Giannelli realized, his nineteen years of experience focused on this second—of an arsonist's work. The other thing Giannelli noticed as he headed for the building was a curious sound. Over the roar of trucks, of water being dumped into the front of the building, over the sirens going and men shouting, he heard faint, high-pitched cries that sounded a little like meows. And the driver getting out of the engine truck next to him heard it, too. "Where the heck is it coming from?" he said as both surveyed the chaos around them.

Giannelli approached the front of the building, where men were already pouring as much water as they could on the fire without getting any closer than fifteen feet, and he still heard the mewing. He went up to the lieutenant. There was nothing he could do, after all, with no windows to vent or second floors to crawl through, and some thirty firefighters on the scene. So he said to his boss, as he's known to do whenever there's the possibility of an animal in danger, "You don't need me standing here, right?"

The lieutenant nodded. "Go ahead," he said. And Giannelli started to look around. He followed his ears to the side of the two-story brick building next door, and the noises got louder. There in front of him were three stray kittens, hunkered against the wall, quivering and crying, maybe a little in shock, too. So that was it. "Get me a box," he called to a bystander, and gingerly lifted each one into it. They weighed next to nothing. All were scorched, their fur smoky, and the ears of some were a little singed.

In the box, they huddled close and cried, but Giannelli had to get back to the fire. A man from the neighborhood was walking by. "Here," Giannelli said, "take this down the street?" The man agreed.

"Take it to the porch, then," Giannelli told him. "Not the one next door, but the one after that." If anything happened to make this fire leap into action again, he wanted the kittens as far away as possible. He didn't know what they'd been through, but it couldn't have been good.

Back at the front of the garage, the fire was dying down, leaving billowing smoke as its good-bye. The snow was still falling as the morning sun rose and the firemen, the pressure off them, hung around watching the garage smolder. "Three kittens," he told them, as if it were over. But then he heard something else.

"How could there be more in the middle of all this?" another firefighter said. But firemen don't speculate, they search. So Giannelli and a few others took another look.

Across the street, pressed against the blacktop in an empty space next to the curb, was a tiny asphalt-colored kitten. Giannelli picked it up, then saw another one, a black-and-white, a few yards away in the patch of grass running between the curb and the sidewalk. It was as if they'd landed in a straight line. And when he followed that line back, he landed on the place where he'd found the first three kittens.

Somewhere, he realized, must be the mother cat. The reason he'd found the kittens in this arrangement was because she'd been carrying them away from the fire, one by one. Considering how smoky and scorched they were, that could only mean one thing. She'd not only carried them out of the fire, she'd gone back into the flames, again and again, to get them. Which meant that wherever she was, she was in rough shape, if not dead. If she'd even made it back out of the garage.

# SCARLETT SAVES HER FAMILY

A couple of guys, including a cop from the 75th Precinct, helped Giannelli look. Someone said he'd seen a cat running to the vacant lot right across the street, beyond the line of her kittens. So she'd been scared away by all the commotion of the fire companies reporting. Or, Giannelli wondered, had she made her rescues while they'd been fighting the fire, right under their feet—and, almost, their wheels?

They hurried over to the vacant lot, and there, behind a pile of rubble, was the mother cat. She wasn't moving, and she had been badly burned. He bent down to scoop her up.

"Be careful," the cop next to him said. "She might be nasty. She might try to scratch."

"I don't think so," Giannelli said. And then, upon closer look, his heart broke.

Her eyes were blistered shut, her mouth, ears, and face scorched, her coat badly singed. Her paws were crusted with thick black soot. But this little cat was alive. Her pain unleashed from being moved, she opened her mouth in a silent protest, then seemed to change her mind and just lay, unmoving, in the fireman's arms.

Giannelli held her close against his chest and tried to figure out what to do. The snow was falling harder. His men were stowing their gear on the truck, almost ready to leave. The little gray runt and the black-and-white kitten were with their three siblings in the box on the porch, and if he didn't do something fast, their mother would probably die. At the same time, he was imagining what must have happened. He pictured this scrawny street cat, pressing closer to the ground as she smelled smoke and sensed the danger, feeling the overwhelming urge to run. Cats, he knew, tended to crouch in a corner, trying to hide from the flames until the last minute and then making a wild dash for safety. But she was also a mother cat, a nursing cat. So as this urge to run was blaring loudly in her mind, something else called even louder. Maternal instinct? It had sent her into probable death, into a rage of smoke and flames, had sent her racing over burning embers again and again. Five times. Five kittens. At the very least, she should be united with her litter.

When he reached the box of kittens on the neighbor's porch, he carefully placed their mother among them. What happened next was a gift. The kittens started mewing, excited to have their mother back. Even in the shape she was in, however exhausted and hurt she was, she did what a mother cat does. Though her eyes were swollen shut, she circled wobbily among them, pressing her nose against each of them in turn, inhaling each one's scent, making a sightless head count. And then, finally, she lay down among them so they would feel safe in the haven of the deep cardboard box, and started to purr. It was faint and it was a little rough on the edges. But Giannelli knew. Satisfied they were all there, the mother cat purred with relief.

# CAT FACTS

  ✳ Cats rarely meow at other cats. They only meow at us!

 ✳ In ancient Egypt, cats were so revered that whenever a cat passed away, its owners would shave their eyebrows as a symbol of mourning.

  ✳ Did you know that cats actually walk on their toes, not their feet?

 ✳ The smallest cat on record was a male Himalayan-Persian mix from Illinois named Tinker Toy. Fully grown, he reached only 2 3/4 inches tall and 7 1/4 inches long.

✳A  c a t  c a n  j u m p  5  t i m e s

 ✳ Cats spend 2/3 of their lifetime sleeping— that's about 16 hours every day!

 ✳ Just like the human fingerprint, no two cats have the same ridged pattern on their nose pad.

* Cats can see up to 120 feet away with only ¹/₆ of the light needed by humans.

* A cat drinks by lapping fluid up from the bottom of its tongue. Is that like drinking a glass of water upside down?

* The heart of a cat beats twice as fast as the heart of a human.

# higher than its actual height!

* The largest cat on record was an Australian feline named Himmy. He reached the amazing weight of 46 pounds, 15.25 ounces!

* There are over 500 million domestic cats in the world!!!

# THE CAT LADY

*BY Q. K.*

There's something most mysterious
    about old Widow Brown;
The little house she lives in is
    the oddest in the town.
It's tucked amongst the others
    where it seems to try to hide,
And its funny wee roof-garden has
    a tree on either side.

At eight o'clock each morning,
    neither after nor before,
I'm sure to see old Mrs. Brown
    appearing at her door,
And then we stand and watch the
    sight that both of us expect—
As if a spell attracted them the
    eager cats collect.

When I was little I supposed that
    Mrs. Brown must be
A witch, who summoned crowds of
    cats in such variety
To make them do her wicked will—
    enchanted cats, no doubt—
To bring her news from all the world
    and carry tales about.

That she had put a charm on them,
    I found at last, is true;
To make them gather round her door
    in dozens as they do.
It's quite a simple, harmless charm,
    not difficult to teach—
She's given, every day for years,
    a bit of fish to each!

# CAT TREATS

Just for cats, this delectable kitty snack is not for everyday feeding. But for special occasions, such as feline birthdays or anniversaries, its *purr*fect.

½ can sardines, drained

1 cup plain bread crumbs

1 tablespoon vegetable oil

1 egg, beaten

1. Preheat oven to 350° F.

2. In a medium size bowl, mash the sardines with a fork into little pieces.

3. Add remaining ingredients and mix well.

4. Roll into little balls (the size of marbles) and drop on to a greased cookie sheet (or one lined with parchment paper).

5. Bake for 8 minutes.

6. Cool to room temperature and store in an airtight container in the refrigerator.

*A True Story*

# HE WAS A GOOD LION

*BY BERYL MARKHAM*

*In this story, excerpted from her memoir,* West with the Night, *Beryl Markham tells of her face-to-face encounter with a lion while growing up in Africa.*

There was a place called Elkington's Farm by Kabete Station. It was near Nairobi on the edge of the Kikuyu Reserve, and my father and I used to ride there from town on horses or in a buggy, and along the way my father would tell me stories about Africa.

One day, when we were riding to Elkington's, my father spoke about lions.

"Lions are more intelligent than some men," he said, "and more courageous than most. A lion will fight for what he has and for what he needs; he is contemptuous of cowards and wary of his equals. But he is not afraid. You can always trust a lion to be exactly what it is—and never anything else.

"Except," he added, looking more paternally concerned than usual, "that damned lion of Elkington's!"

The Elkington lion was famous within a radius of twelve miles in all directions from the farm, because, if you happened to be anywhere inside that circle,

204

you could hear him roar when he was hungry, when he was sad, or when he just felt like roaring. If, in the night, you lay sleepless on your bed and listened to an intermittent sound that began like the bellow of a banshee trapped in the bowels of Kilimanjaro and ended like the sound of that same banshee suddenly at large and arrived at the foot of your bed, you knew (because you had been told) that this was the song of Paddy.

Two or three of the settlers in East Africa at that time had caught lion cubs and raised them in cages. But Paddy, the Elkington lion, had never seen a cage.

He had grown to full size, tawny, black-maned, and muscular, without a worry or a care. He lived on fresh meat, not of his own killing. He spent his waking hours (which coincided with everybody else's sleeping hours) wandering through Elkington's fields and pastures like an affable, if apostrophic, emperor, a-stroll in the gardens of his court.

He thrived on solitude. He had no mate, but pretended indifference and walked alone, not toying too much with imaginings of the unattainable. There were no physical barriers to his freedom, but the lions of the plains do not accept into their respected fraternity an individual bearing in his coat the smell of men. So Paddy ate, slept, and roared, and perhaps he sometimes dreamed, but he never left Elkington's. He was a tame lion, Paddy was. He was deaf to the call of the wild.

# HE WAS A GOOD LION

"I'm always careful of that lion," I told my father, "but he's really harmless. I have seen Mrs. Elkington stroke him."

"Which proves nothing," said my father. "A domesticated lion is only an unnatural lion—and whatever is unnatural is untrustworthy."

Whenever my father made an observation as deeply philosophical as that one, and as inclusive, I knew there was nothing more to be said.

I nudged my horse and we broke into a canter covering the remaining distance to Elkington's.

It wasn't a big farm as farms went in Africa before the First World War, but it had a very nice house with a large veranda on which my father, Jim Elkington, Mrs. Elkington, and one or two other settlers sat and talked with what to my mind was always unreasonable solemnity.

There were drinks, but beyond that there was a tea table lavishly spread, as only the English can spread them. I have sometimes thought since of the Elkingtons' tea table—round, capacious, and white, standing with sturdy legs against the green vines of the garden, a thousand miles of Africa receding from its edge.

As I scampered past the square hay shed a hundred yards or so behind the Elkington house, I caught sight of Bishon Singh, whom my father had sent ahead to tend our horses.

# HE WAS A GOOD LION

He raised his arm and greeted me in Swahili as I ran through the Elkington farmyard and out toward the open country.

Why I ran at all or with what purpose is beyond my answering, but when I had no specific destination I always ran as fast as I could in the hope of finding one—and I always found it.

I was within twenty yards of the Elkington lion before I saw him. He lay sprawled in the morning sun, huge, black-maned, and gleaming with life. His tail moved slowly, stroking the rough grass like a knotted rope end. His body was sleek and easy, making a mold where he lay, a cool mold, that would be there when he had gone. He was not asleep; he was only idle. He was rusty-red, and soft, like a strokable cat. I stopped and he lifted his head with magnificent ease and stared at me out of yellow eyes.

I stood there staring back, scuffling my bare toes in the dust, pursing my lips to make a noiseless whistle—a very small girl who knew nothing about lions.

Paddy raised himself then, emitting a little sigh, and began to contemplate me with a kind of quiet premeditation, like that of a slow-witted man fondling an unaccustomed thought.

I cannot say that there was any menace in his eyes, because there wasn't, or that his "frightful jowls" were drooling, because they were handsome jowls and very tidy. He did sniff the air, though, with what impressed me as being close to audible satisfaction. And he did not lie down again.

I remembered the rules that one remembers. I did not run. I walked very slowly, and I began to sing a defiant song.

"*Kali coma Simba sisi,*" I sang. "*Askari yoti ni udari!*— Fierce like the lion are we, Askari all are brave!"

I went in a straight line past Paddy when I sang it, seeing his eyes shine in the thick grass, watching his tail beat time to the meter of my ditty.

"*Twendi, twendi—ku pigana—pigana aduoi—piga sana!*—Let us go, let us go—to fight—beat down the enemy! Beat hard, beat hard!"

What lion would not be impressed with the marching song of the King's African Rifles?

Singing it still, I took up my trot toward the rim of the low hill that might, if I were lucky, have Cape gooseberry bushes on its slopes.

The country was gray-green and dry, and the sun lay on it closely, making the ground hot under my bare feet. There was no sound and no wind.

Even Paddy made no sound, coming swiftly behind me.

What I remember most clearly of the moment that followed are three things—a scream that was barely a whisper, a blow that struck me to the ground, and, as I buried my face in my arms and felt Paddy's teeth close on the flesh of my leg, a fantastically bobbing turban, that was Bishon Singh's turban, appear over the edge of the hill.

I remained conscious, but I closed my eyes and tried not to be. It was not so much the pain as it was the sound.

The sound of Paddy's roar in my ears will only be duplicated, I think, when the doors of hell slip their wobbly hinges, one day, and give voice and authenticity to the whole panorama of Dante's poetic nightmares. It was an immense roar that encompassed the world and dissolved me in it.

I shut my eyes very tight, and lay still under the weight of Paddy's paws.

Bishon Singh said afterward that he did nothing. He said he had remained by the hay shed for a few minutes after I ran past him, and then, for no explainable reason had begun to follow me. He admitted, though, that a little while before, he had seen Paddy go in the direction I had taken.

The Sikh called for help, of course, when he saw the lion meant to attack, and a half dozen of Elkington's syces had come running from the house. Along with them had come Jim Elkington with a rawhide whip.

It happened like this—as Bishon Singh told it:

"I am resting against the walls of the place where hay is kept and first the large lion and then you, Beru, pass me going toward the open field, and a thought comes to me that a lion and a young girl are strange company, so I follow. I follow to the place where the hill that goes up becomes the hill that goes down, and where it goes down deepest I see that you are running without much thought in your head, and the lion is running behind you with many thoughts in his head, and I scream for everybody to come very fast.

"Everybody comes very fast, but the large lion is faster than anybody, and he jumps on your back and I see you scream but I hear no scream. I only hear the lion, and I begin to run with everybody and this included Bwana Elkington, who is saying a great many words I do not know and is carrying a long kiboko which he is holding in his hand and is meant for beating the large lion.

"Bwana Elkington goes past me the way a man with lighter legs and fewer inches around his stomach might go past me, and he is waving the long kiboko so that it whistles over all our heads like a very sharp wind, but when we get close to the lion it comes to my mind that the lion is not of the mood to accept a kilboko.

"He is standing with the front of himself on your back, Beru, and you are bleeding in three or five places, and he is roaring. I do not believe Bwana Elkington could have thought that that lion at that moment would consent to being beaten, because the lion was not looking the way he had ever looked before when it was necessary for him to be beaten. He was looking as if he did not wish to be disturbed by a kiboko, or the Bwana, or the syces, or Bishon Singh, and he was saying so in a very large voice.

"I believe that Bwana Elkington understood this voice when he was still more than several feet from the lion, and I believe that Bwana considered in his mind that it would be the best thing not to beat the lion just then, but the Bwana when he runs very fast is like the trunk of a great baobab tree rolling down a slope, and it seems that because of this it was not possible for him to explain the thought of his mind to the soles of his feet in a sufficient quickness of time to prevent him from rushing much closer to the lion than in his heart he wished to be.

"And it was in this circumstance, as I am telling it," said Bishon Singh, "which in my considered opinion made it possible for you to be alive, Beru."

"Bwana Elkington rushed at the lion then, Bishon Singh?"

"The lion, as of the contrary, rushed at Bwana Elkington," said Bishon Singh. "The lion deserted you for the Bwana, Beru. The lion was of the opinion that his master was not in any way deserving of a portion of what he, the lion, had accomplished in the matter of fresh meat through no effort by anybody except himself."

Bishon Singh offered this extremely reasonable interpretation with impressive gravity, as if he were expounding the Case for the Lion to a chosen jury of Paddy's peers.

"Fresh meat . . . ," I repeated dreamily, and crossed my fingers.

"So then what happened . . . ?"

The Sikh lifted his shoulders and let them drop again. "What could happen, Beru? The lion rushed for Bwana Elkington, who in his turn rushed from the lion, and in so rushing did not keep in his hand the long kiboko, but allowed it to fall upon the ground, and in accomplishing this the Bwana was free to ascend a very fortunate tree, which he did."

"And you picked me up, Bishon Singh?"

He made a little dip with his massive turban. "I was happy with the duty of carrying you back to this very bed, Beru, and of advising your father, who had gone to observe some of Bwana Elkington's horses, that you had been moderately eaten by the large lion. Your father returned very fast, and Bwana Elkington some time later returned very fast, but the large lion has not returned at all."

The large lion had not returned at all. That night he killed a horse, and the next night he killed a yearling bullock, and after that a cow fresh for milking.

In the end he was caught and finally caged, but brought to no rendezvous with the firing squad at sunrise. He remained for years in his cage, which, had he managed to live in freedom with his inhibitions, he might never have seen at all.

He was a good lion. He had done what he could about being a tame lion. Who thinks it just to be judged by a single error?

I still have the scars of his teeth and claws, but they are very small now and almost forgotten, and I cannot begrudge him his moment.

# ANIMAL MAKEOVERS

**W**e may be higher on the food chain, but no one has more fun than our animal friends. After all, have you ever seen a lion doing homework, or a dog eating vegetables? So the next time you're in the mood to take a break from being you, try one of these nifty makeovers. It's the perfect way to step into the skin of your favorite furry beast. Crouch like a cheetah prowling the African jungle! Roll around on the floor like a pig in a mud puddle! Bark like a seal after a fresh catch of fish! The choice is all yours. Just close your eyes and ask yourself: What animal do I want to be today…?

# Paper Plate Masks

paper plate, scissors, crayons,
construction paper, glue, hole punch, yarn

*optional*: tissue paper, glitter, pipe cleaners

1. With the help of an adult, place a clean paper plate over your face and mark where your eyes should go. Cut out your peepholes.

2. Using crayons, start drawing the animal face onto the mask. Remember that almost all animals have a mouth, whether it's a lion's bearded scowl, or a pair of insect mandibles.

3. Draw in a nose. Add some hairs if you are a mammal, scales if you are feeling reptilian, or feathers to fluff in the birdbath. Pipe cleaners and glue make for good whiskers. Ears, jaws, and tongues can be made from construction paper, and the bottoms of egg cartons create great buggy eyes. Colored yarn also serves as a nice furry mane.

4. When you finish decorating, punch a hole on either side of the mask. String two pieces of yarn through the holes and knot them in place. To wear your mask, tie both ends together behind your head. Instant MANIMAL!

# Animal Ears Headbands

ribbon, construction paper, scissors; colored crayons,
markers, or pencils; tape or a stapler

*optional:* glue, cotton balls, yarn

1. Use a piece of ribbon to measure the circumference of your head.

2. To make the headband, cut a 2 to 3-inch-wide strip of construction paper (the same length as the ribbon plus an extra inch).

3. From another piece of construction paper, cut out the ear shapes of your favorite animal. For example, cat ears are short and pointy; bear or mouse ears are short and rounded; dog ears are either short and upright or long and floppy; elephant ears are large and rounded; and rabbit ears are long and oval.

4. Color and decorate your ears using your markers and crayons. For example, add stripes if you are a tiger or a tabby cat, spots if you're a leopard or a dalmatian dog, or cotton balls to make your bunny ears soft and fuzzy. You can even add some fur to your headband by gluing on short pieces of colored yarn.

5. Tape or staple the bottom of your animal ears to the inside of the headband. Floppy ears, like those of an elephant or a cocker spaniel, should hang down, while alert ears, like those of a zebra or cat, should be upright.

6. Tape or staple the ends of the paper headband together, overlapping one inch.

7. Slide the headband over the top of your head. It should fit snugly around your forehead.

# LITTLE BUNNY FOO FOO

Lit - tle Bun - ny Foo - Foo, Hop-ping thru the for - est,

Scoop-ing up the field mice and bop-pin' 'em on the head.

*Spoken:*

Down came the good fair - y And she said:

"Lit - tle Bun - ny Foo - Foo, I don't want to see you

Scoop-ing up the field mice and bop-pin' 'em on the head.

*Spoken:*

I'll give you three chan-ces, And if you don't be-have,

I'll turn you in - to a goon!"

*Spoken:* The next day:

2. Same as verse 1 except on line 6,
"I'll give you two more chances..."

3. "I'll give you one more chance..."

4. "I gave you three chances and you
didn't behave. Now you're a goon!
POOF!!"

# THE VELVETEEN RABBIT

## OR

## HOW TOYS BECOME REAL

### BY MARGERY WILLIAMS

There was once a velveteen rabbit, and in the beginning he was really splendid. He was fat and bunchy, as a rabbit should be; his coat was spotted brown and white, he had real thread whiskers, and his ears were lined with pink sateen. On Christmas morning, when he sat wedged in the top of the Boy's stocking, with a sprig of holly between his paws, the effect was charming.

There were other things in the stocking, nuts and oranges and a toy engine, and chocolate almonds and a clockwork mouse, but the Rabbit was quite the best of all. For at least two hours the Boy loved him, and then Aunts and Uncles came to dinner, and there was a great rustling of tissue paper and unwrapping of parcels, and in the excitement of looking at all the new presents the Velveteen Rabbit was forgotten.

For a long time he lived in the toy cupboard or on the nursery floor, and no one thought very much about him.

The Skin Horse had lived longer in the nursery than any of the others. He was so old that his brown coat was bald in patches and showed the seams underneath, and most of the hairs in

his tail had been pulled out to string bead necklaces. He was wise, for he had seen a long succession of mechanical toys arrive to boast and swagger, and by-and-by break their mainsprings and pass away, and he knew that they were only toys, and would never turn into anything else. For nursery magic is very strange and wonderful, and only those playthings that are old and wise and experienced like the Skin Horse understand all about it.

"What is REAL?" asked the Rabbit one day, when they were lying side by side near the nursery fender, before Nana came to tidy the room. "Does it mean having things that buzz inside you and a stick-out handle?"

"Real isn't how you are made," said the Skin Horse. "It's a thing that happens to you. When a child loves you for a long, long time, not just to play with, but REALLY loves you, then you become Real."

"Does it hurt?" asked the Rabbit.

"Sometimes," said the Skin Horse, for he was always truthful. "When you are Real you don't mind being hurt."

"Does it happen all at once, like being wound up," he asked, "or bit by bit?"

"It doesn't happen all at once," said the Skin Horse. "You become. It takes a long time. That's why it doesn't often happen to people who break easily, or have sharp edges, or who have to be carefully kept. Generally, by the time you are Real, most of your hair has been loved off, and your eyes drop out and you get loose in the joints and very shabby. But these things don't matter at all, because once you are Real you can't be ugly, except to people who don't understand."

# THE VELVETEEN RABBIT

"I suppose you are Real?" said the Rabbit. And then he wished he had not said it, for he thought the Skin Horse might be sensitive. But the Skin Horse only smiled.

"The Boy's Uncle made me Real," he said. "That was a great many years ago; but once you are Real you can't become unreal again. It lasts for always."

The Rabbit sighed. He thought it would be a long time before this magic called Real happened to him. He longed to become Real, to know what it felt like; and yet the idea of growing shabby and losing his eyes and whiskers was rather sad. He wished that he could become it without these uncomfortable things happening to him.

There was a person called Nana who ruled the nursery. Sometimes she took no notice of the playthings lying about, and sometimes, for no reason whatever, she went swooping about like a great wind and hustled them away in cupboards. She called this "tidying up," and the playthings all hated it, especially the tin ones. The Rabbit didn't mind it so much, for wherever he was thrown he came down soft.

One evening, when the Boy was going to bed, he couldn't find the china dog that always slept with him. Nana was in a hurry, and it was too much trouble to hunt for china dogs at bedtime, so she simply looked about her, and seeing that the toy cupboard door stood open, she made a swoop.

"Here," she said, "take your old Bunny! He'll do to sleep with you!" And she dragged the Rabbit out by one ear, and put him into the Boy's arms.

That night, and for many nights after, the Velveteen Rabbit slept in the Boy's bed. At first he found it rather uncomfortable, for the Boy hugged him very tight, and sometimes he rolled over on him, and sometimes he pushed him so far under the pillow that the Rabbit could scarcely breathe. And he missed, too, those long moonlight hours in the nursery, when all the house was silent, and his talks with the Skin Horse. But very soon he grew to like it, for the Boy used to talk to him, and made nice tunnels for him under the bedclothes that he said were like the burrows the real rabbits lived in. And they had splendid games together, in whispers, when Nana had gone away to her supper and left the nightlight burning on the mantelpiece. And when the Boy dropped off

224

to sleep, the Rabbit would snuggle down close under his little warm chin and dream, with the Boy's hands clasped close round him all night long.

And so time went on, and the little Rabbit was very happy—so happy that he never noticed how his beautiful velveteen fur was getting shabbier and shabbier, and his tail was coming unsewn, and all the pink rubbed off his nose where the Boy had kissed him.

Spring came, and they had long days in the garden, for wherever the Boy went the Rabbit went too. He had rides in the wheelbarrow, and picnics on the grass, and lovely fairy huts built for him under the raspberry canes behind the flower border. And once, when the Boy was called away suddenly to go out to tea, the Rabbit was left out on the lawn until long after dusk, and Nana had to come and look for him with the candle because the Boy couldn't go to sleep unless he was there. He was wet through with the dew and quite earthy from diving into the burrows the Boy had made for him in the flower bed, and Nana grumbled as she rubbed him off with a corner of her apron.

"You must have your old Bunny!" she said. "Fancy all that fuss for a toy!"

The Boy sat up in bed and stretched out his hands.

"Give me my Bunny!" he said. "You mustn't say that. He isn't a toy. He's REAL!"

When the little Rabbit heard that he was happy, for he knew that what the Skin Horse had said was true at last. The nursery magic had happened to him, and he was a toy no longer. He was Real. The Boy himself had said it.

# Animal Scramblers

Unscramble the letters to spell the name of an animal.

Once you've solved all of these, try making up some of your own to stump your friends. Just write down a list of your favorite animals and mix up the letters.

1. GRALLITOA

2. OKNAROGA

3. ESOMO

4. SONRIDAU

5. HNTPALEE

6. DRIMIHMBUNG

7. ARIOLGL

8. LIRYEFF

9. EEKSRTLATAN

10. ORLADEP

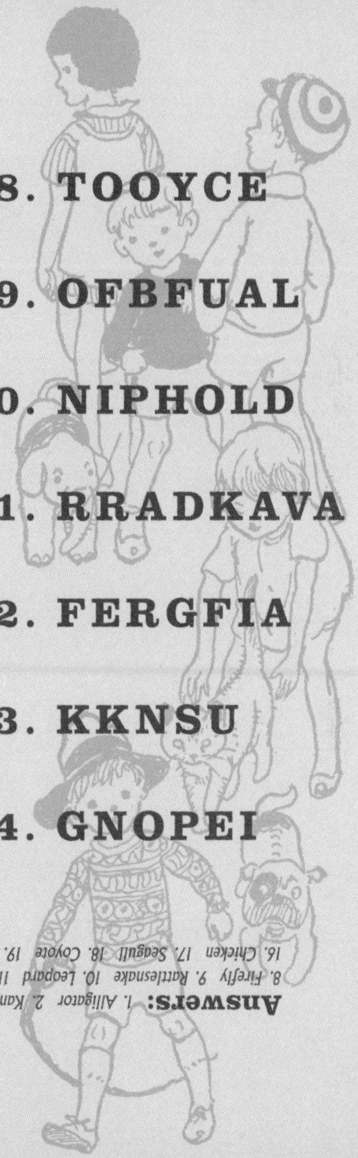

11. TROGNAUNA

12. MELAHCNEO

13. GOGRUDNOH

14. ICLEERTC ELE

15. BLERTSO

16. CNEHKIC

17. LESLUAG

18. TOOYCE

19. OFBFUAL

20. NIPHOLD

21. RRADKAVA

22. FERGFIA

23. KKNSU

24. GNOPEI

**Answers:** 1. Alligator 2. Kangaroo 3. Moose 4. Dinosaur 5. Elephant 6. Hummingbird 7. Gorilla 8. Firefly 9. Rattlesnake 10. Leopard 11. Orangutan 12. Chameleon 13. Groundhog 14. Electric eel 15. Lobster 16. Chicken 17. Seagull 18. Coyote 19. Buffalo 20. Dolphin 21. Aardvark 22. Giraffe 23 Skunk 24. Pigeon

# AN EXCITING STORY

BY CATHERINE A. MORIN

*Peg.*

Now, you lie there, my dear Maria,
I'll sit down here, beside the fire,
And have a jolly read till tea.

*Pup.*
*[sniffing]*

(*This* book, of course, is meant for me.)

*Peg.*

"High on the hills the castle stood,
Below, lay the enchanted wood,
So dark, you couldn't see a wink—

*Pup.*
*[licking]*

(I quite enjoy the taste of ink!)

*Peg.*
*[still reading]*

"A dragon lurked there in the gloom.
The Princess pined within her room,
Up many a long and winding stair—"

*Pup.*
*[chewing]*

(How *lovely* paper is to tear!)

| | |
|---|---|
| *Peg.* | Oh! This is really quite excitin', |
| | The kind of tale I just delight in! |
| | Let's see what comes, when I turn over. |
| *Pup.* | (I'll have a go now at the cover.) |
| | |
| *Peg.* | "There came a fearful roaring sound, |
| *[reading]* | It seemed to shake the very ground; |
| | And then a voice cried, grim and gruff—" |
| *Pup.* | (Woof! Woof! At last I've got it off!) |
| *[getting excited]* | |
| | |
| *Peg.* | Whatever are you doing, Pup? |
| *[jumping up]* | You *naughty* dog! You've torn in up! |
| *Pup.* | Woof! Woof! Of course—great pains I took. |
| *[wagging his tail]* | I *do* enjoy a story book! |

232

# DOG BISCUITS

**J**ust for dogs, these delicious treats are like the canine version of a peanut butter and honey sandwich... Yum!

*1 tablespoon honey*

*1 teaspoon peanut butter*

*¾ cup flour*

*1 egg*

*¼ cup vegetable oil*

*1 teaspoon baking soda*

*¼ cup rolled oats*

*½ teaspoon vanilla*

1. Preheat oven to 350° F.

2. In a medium size, microwave-safe bowl, mix together honey and peanut butter.

3. Heat honey-and-peanut butter mixture in microwave for about 20 seconds or until runny.

4. Add remaining ingredients and mix well.

5. Spoon mixture, one teaspoon at a time, onto a greased cookie sheet (or one lined with parchment paper). Place each scoop 2 inches apart.

6. Bake for 8 to 10 minutes.

7. Remove and cool. Store in an airtight container.

*Makes 45 to 50 biscuits*

# LASSIE COME-HOME

### BY ERIC KNIGHT

The dog had met the boy by the school gate for five years. Now she couldn't understand that times were changed and she wasn't supposed to be there any more. But the boy knew.

So when he opened the door of the cottage, he spoke before he entered.

"Mother," he said, "Lassie's come home again."

He waited a moment, as if in hope of something. But the man and woman inside the cottage did not speak.

"Come in, Lassie," the boy said.

He held open the door, and the tri-color collie walked in obediently. Going head down, as a collie will when it knows something is wrong, it went to the rug and lay down before the hearth, a black-white-and-gold aristocrat. The man, sitting on a low stool by the fireside, kept his eyes turned away. The woman went to the sink and busied herself there.

"She were waiting at school for me, just like always," the boy went on. He spoke fast, as if racing against time. "She must ha' got away again. I thought, happen this time, we might just—"

"No!" the woman exploded.

The boy's carelessness dropped. His voice rose in pleading.

"But this time, mother! Just this time. We could hide her. They wouldn't never know."...

"Well, she's sold, so ye can take her out o' my house and home to them as bought her!"

The boy's bottom lip crept out stubbornly, and there was silence in the cottage. Then the dog lifted its head and nudged the man's hand, as a dog will when asking for patting. But the man drew away and stared, silently, into the fire.

The boy tried again, with the ceaseless guile of a child, his voice coaxing.

"Look, feyther, she wants thee to bid her welcome. Aye, she's that glad to be home. Happen they don't tak'

good care on her up there? Look, her coat's a bit poorly, don't ye think? A bit o' linseed strained through her drinking water—that's what I'd gi' her."

Still looking in the fire, the man nodded. But the woman, as if perceiving the boy's new attack, sniffed....

"My gum, she is off a bit," the woman said. Then she caught herself. "Ma goodness, I suppose I'll have to fix her a bit o' summat. She can do wi' it. But soon as she's fed, back she goes. And never another dog I'll have in my house. Never another. Cooking and nursing for 'em, and as much trouble to bring up as a bairn!"

So, grumbling and chattering as a village woman will, she moved about, warming a pan of food for the dog. The man and boy watched the collie eat. When it was done, the boy took from the mantelpiece a folded cloth and a brush, and began prettying the collie's coat. The man watched for several minutes, and then could stand it no longer.

"Here," he said.

He took the cloth and brush from the boy and began working expertly on the dog, rubbing the rich, deep coat, then brushing the snowy whiteness of the full ruff and the apron, bringing out the heavy leggings on the forelegs. He lost himself in his work, and the boy sat on the rug, watching contentedly. The woman stood it as long as she could.

"Now will ye please tak' that tyke out o' here?"

The man flared in anger.

"Well, ye wouldn't have me tak' her back looking like a mucky Monday wash, wouldta?"

He bent again, and began fluffing out the collie's petticoats.

"Joe!" the woman pleaded. "Will ye tak' her out o' here? Hynes'll be nosing round afore ye know it. And I won't have that man in my house. Wearing his hat inside, and going on like he's the duke himself—him and his leggings!"

"All right, lass."

"And this time, Joe, tak' young Joe wi' ye."

"What for?"

"Well, let's get the business done and over with. It's him that Lassie runs away for. She comes for young Joe. So if he went wi' thee, and told her to stay, happen she'd be content and not run away no more, and then we'd have a little peace and quiet in the home— though heaven knows there's not much hope o' that these days, things being like they are." The woman's voice trailed away, as if she would soon cry in weariness.

# LASSIE COME-HOME

The man rose. "Come, Joe," he said. "Get thy cap."

The Duke of Rudling walked along the gravel paths of his place with his granddaughter, Philippa....

"Country going to pot!" the duke roared, stabbing at the walk with his great blackthorn stick. "When I was a young man! Hah! Women today not as pretty. Horses today not as fast. As for dogs—ye don't see dogs today like—"

Just then the duke and Philippa came round a clump of rhododendrons and saw a man, a boy and a dog.

"Ah," said the duke, in admiration. Then his brow knotted. "Damme, Carraclough! What're ye doing with my dog?"...

"It's Lassie," Carraclough said. "She runned away again and I brought her back ...."

"Damme, ran away again!" the duke roared. "And I told that utter nincompoop Hynes to—where is he? Hynes! Hynes! Damme, Hynes, what're ye hiding for?"

"Coming, your lordship!" sounded a voice, far away behind the shrubberies. And soon Hynes appeared, a sharp-faced man in check coat, riding breeches, and the cloth leggings that grooms wear.

"Take this dog," roared the duke, "and pen her up! And, damme, if she breaks out again, I'll—I'll—"

The duke waved his great stick threateningly, and then, without so much as a thank you or kiss the back of my hand to Joe Carraclough, he went stamping and muttering away.

"I'll pen 'er up," Hynes muttered, when the duke was gone. "And if she ever gets away agyne, I'll—"

# LASSIE COME-HOME

He made as if to grab the dog, but Joe Carraclough's hobnailed boot trod heavily on Hynes' foot.

"I brought my lad wi' me to bid her stay, so we'll pen her up this time. Eigh—sorry! I didn't see I were on thy foot. Come, Joe, lad."

They walked down the crunching gravel path, along by the neat kennel buildings. When Lassie was behind the closed door, she raced into the high wire run where she could see them as they went. She pressed close against the wire, waiting.

The boy stood close too, his fingers through the meshes touching the dog's nose.

"Go on, lad," his father ordered. "Bid her stay!"

The boy looked around, as if for help that he did not find. He swallowed, and then spoke, low and quickly.

"Stay here, Lassie, and don't come home no more," he said. "And don't come to school for me no more. Because I don't want to see you no more. 'Cause tha's a bad dog, and we don't love thee no more, and we don't want thee. So stay there forever and leave us be, and don't never come home no more."...

After that, there were days and days that passed, and the dog did not come to the school gate any more. So then it was not like old times. There were so many things that were not like old times.

The boy was thinking that as he came wearily up the path and opened the cottage door and heard his father's voice, tense with anger: "... walk my feet off. If tha thinks I like—"

Then they heard his opening of the door and the voice stopped and the cottage was silent.

243

# LASSIE COME-HOME

That's how it was now, the boy thought. They stopped talking in front of you. And this, somehow, was too much for him to bear.

He closed the door, ran out into the night, and onto the moor, that great flat expanse of land where all the people of that village walked in lonesomeness when life and its troubles seemed past bearing.

A long while later, his father's voice cut through the darkness.

"What's tha doing out here, Joe lad?"

"Walking."

"Aye."

They went on together, aimlessly, each following his own thoughts. And they both thought about the dog that had been sold.

"Tha maun't think we're hard on thee, Joe," the man said at last. "It's just that a chap's got to be honest. There's that to it. Sometimes, when a chap doesn't have much, he clings right hard to what he's got. And honest is honest, and there's no two ways about it."...

"But Lassie was—"

"Now, Joe! Ye can't alter it, ever. It's done—and happen, it's for t' best. No two ways, Joe, she were getting hard to feed. Why, ye wouldn't want Lassie to be going around getting peaked and pined, like some chaps round here keep their tykes. And if ye're fond of her, then just think on it that now she's got lots to eat, and a private kennel, and a good run to herself, and living like a varritable princess, she is. Ain't that best for her?"

"We wouldn't pine her. We've always got lots to eat."

The man blew out his breath, angrily. "Eigh, Joe, nowt pleases thee.

# LASSIE COME-HOME

Well then, tha might as well have it. Tha'll never see Lassie no more. She run home once too often, so the duke's taken her wi' him up to his place in Scotland, and there she'll stay. So it's good-by and good luck to her, and she'll never come home no more, she won't. Now, I weren't off to tell thee, but there it is, so put it in thy pipe and smoke it, and let's never say a word about it no more—especially in front of thy mother."...

Then they were quiet, until, over the rise, they saw the lights of the village. Then the boy spoke: How far away is Scotland, feyther?"

"Nay, lad, it's a long, long road."

"But how far, feyther?"

"I don't know—but it's a longer road than thee or me'll ever walk...."

Joe Carraclough was right. It is a long road, as they say in the North, from Yorkshire to Scotland. Much too far for a man to walk—or a boy. And though the boy often thought of it, he remembered his father's words on the moor, and he put the thought behind him.

But there is another way of looking at it; and that's the distance from Scotland to Yorkshire. And that is just as far as from Yorkshire to Scotland. A matter of about four hundred miles, it would be, from the Duke of Rudling's place far up in the Highlands, to the village of Holdersby. That would be for a man, who could go fairly straight.

To an animal, how much farther would it be? For a dog can study no maps, read no signposts, ask no directions. It could only go blindly, by instinct, knowing that it must keep on to the south, to the south. It would wander and err, quest and quarter, run into firths and lochs that would send it

245

side-tracking and back-tracking before it could go again on its way—south.

A thousand miles, it would be, going that way—a thousand miles over strange terrain....

And, too, there would be rivers to cross, wide rivers like the Forth and the Clyude, the Tweed and the Tyne, where one must go miles to find bridges. And the bridges would be in towns. And in the towns there would be officials— like the one in Lanarkshire. In all his life he had never let a captured dog get away—except one. That one was a gaunt, snarling collie that whirled on him right in the pound itself, and fought and twisted loose to race away down the city street—going south.

But there are also kind people, too; ones knowing and understanding in the ways of dogs. There was an old couple in Durham who found a dog lying

exhausted in a ditch one night—lying there with its head to the south. They took that dog into their cottage and warmed it and fed it and nursed it....

They tried every wile and every kindness to make it bide with them, but finally, when the dog began to refuse food, the old people knew what they must do. Because they understood dogs, they opened the door one afternoon and they watched a collie go, not down the road to the right, or to the left, but straight across a field toward the south; going steadily at a trot, as if it knew it still had a long, long road to travel.

Ah, a thousand miles of tor and brae, of shire and moor, of path and road and plowland, of river and stream and burn and brook and beck, of snow and rain and fog and sun, is a long way, even for a human being. But it would seem too far—much too far—

for any dog to travel blindly and win through.

And yet—and yet—who shall say why, when so many weeks had passed that hope against hope was dying, a boy coming out of school, out of the cloakroom that always smelled of damp wool drying, across the concrete play yard with the black, waxed slides, should turn his eyes to a spot by the school gate from force of five years of habit, and see there a dog? Not a dog, this one, that lifted glad ears above a proud, slim head with its black-and-gold mask; but a dog that lay weakly, trying to lift a head that would no longer lift, trying to wag a tail that was torn and blotched and matted with dirt and burs, and managing to do nothing much except to whine in a weak, happy, crying way as a boy on his knees threw arms about it, and hands touched it that had not touched it for many a day.

Then who shall picture the urgency of a boy, running, awkwardly, with a great dog in his arms? . . . Or who shall describe the high tones of a voice—a boy's voice, calling as he runs up a path: "Mother! Oh, mother! Lassie's come home! Lassie's come home!"

Nor does any one who ever owned a dog need to be told the sounds a man makes as he bends over a dog that has been his for many years; nor how a woman moves quickly, preparing food—which might be the family's condensed milk stirred into warm water; nor how the jowl of a dog is lifted so that raw egg and brandy, bought with precious pence, should be spooned in; nor how bleeding pads are bandaged, tenderly.

# LASSIE COME-HOME

That was one day. There was another day when the woman in the cottage sighed with pleasure, for a dog lifted itself to its feet for the first time to stand over a bowl of oatmeal, putting its head down and lapping again and again while its pinched flanks quivered.

And there was another day when the boy realized that, even now, the dog was not to be his again. So the cottage rang again with protests and cries, and a woman shrilling: "Is there never to be no more peace in my house and home?" Long after he was in bed that night the boy heard the rise and fall of the woman's voice, and the steady, reiterative tone of the man's. It went on long after he was asleep.

In the morning the man spoke, not looking at the boy, saying the words as if he had long rehearsed them.

"Thy mother and me have decided upon it that Lassie shall stay here till she's better. Anyhow, nobody could nurse her better than us. But the day that t' duke comes back, then back she goes, too. For she belongs to him, and that's honest, too. Now tha has her for a while, so be content."

In childhood, "for a while" is such a great stretch of days when seen from one end. It is a terribly short time seen from the other.

The boy knew how short it was that morning as he went to school and saw a motorcar driven by a young woman. And in the car was a gray-thatched, terrible old man, who waved a cape and shouted: "Hi! Hi, there! Damme, lad! You there! Hi!"...

"Yes, sir."

248

# LASSIE COME-HOME

"You're What's-'is Name's lad, aren't you?"

"Ma feyther's Joe Carraclough."

"I know. I know. Is he home now?"

"No, sir. He's away to Allerby."...

"When'll he be back?"

"I don't know. I think about tea."

"Eh, yes. Well, yes. I'll drop round about fivish to see that father of yours. Something important."

It was hard to pretend to listen to lessons. There was only waiting for noon. Then the boy ran home.

"Mother! T' duke is back and he's coming to take Lassie away."

"Eigh, drat my buttons. Never no peace in this house. Is tha sure?"

"Aye. He stopped me. He said tell feyther he'll be round at five. Can't we hide her? Oh, mother."

"Nay, thy feyther—"

"Won't you beg him? Please, please. Beg feyther to—"

"Young Joe, now it's no use. So stop they teasing! Thy feyther'll not lie. That much I'll give him. Come good, come bad, he'll not lie."

"But just this once, mother. Please beg him, just this once. Just one lie wouldn't hurt him. I'll make it up to him. I will. When I'm growed up, I'll get a job. I'll make money. I'll buy him things—and you, too. I'll buy you both anything you want if you'll only—"

For the first time in his trouble the boy became a child, and the mother, looking over, saw the tears that ran openly down his contorted face. She turned her face to the fire, and there was a pause. Then she spoke.

"Joe, tha mustn't," she said softly. "Tha must learn never to want nothing in life like that. It don't do, lad. Tha mustn't want things bad, like tha wants Lassie."

The boy shook his clenched fists in impatience.

"It ain't that, mother. ye don't understand. Don't ye see—it ain't me that wants her. It's her that wants us! That's what made her come all them miles. It's her that wants us, so terrible bad!"

The woman turned and stared. It was as if, in that moment, she were seeing this child, this boy, this son of her own, for the first time in many years. She turned her head down toward the table. It was surrender.

"Come and eat, then," she said. "I'll talk to him. I will that, all right. I feel sure he won't lie. But I'll talk to him, all right. I'll talk to Mr. Joe Carraclough. I will indeed!"

At five that afternoon, the Duke of Rudling, fuming and muttering, got out of a car at a cottage gate to find a boy barring his way. This was a boy who stood, stubbornly, saying fiercely: "Away wi' thee! Thy tyke's net here!"...

"Why, bless ma heart and sowl," the duke puffed. "Where's thy father, ma lad?"

The door behind the boy opened, and a woman's voice spoke.

"If it's Joe Carraclough ye want, he's out in the shed—and been there shut up half the afternoon."

"What's this lad talking about—a dog of mine being here?"

251

"Nay," the woman snapped quickly. "He didn't say a tyke o' thine was here. He said it wasn't here."

"Well, what dog o' mine isn't here, then?"

The woman swallowed, and looked about as if for help. The duke stood, peering from under his jutting eyebrows. Her answer, truth or lie, was never spoken, for then they heard the rattle of a door opening, and a man making a pursing sound with his lips, as he will when he wants a dog to follow, and then Joe Carraclough's voice said: "This is t' only tyke us has here. Does it look like any dog that belongs to thee?"

With his mough opening to cry one last protest, the boy turned. And his mouth stayed open. For there he saw his father, Joe Carraclough, the collie fancier, standing with a dog at his heels—a dog that sat at his left heel patiently, as any well-trained dog should do—as Lassie used to do. But this dog was not Lassie. In fact, it was ridiculous to think of it at the same moment as you thought of Lassie.

For where Lassie's skull was aristocratic and slim, this dog's head was clumsy and rough. Where Lassie's ears stood in twin-lapped symmetry, this dog had one ear draggling and the other standing up Alsatian fashion in a way to give any collie breeder the cold shivers. Where Lassie's coat was rich tawny gold, this dog's coat had ugly patches of black; and where Lassie's apron was a billowing stretch of snow-white, this dog had puddles of off-color blue-merle mixture. Besides, Lassie had four white paws, and this one had one paw white, two dirty-brown, and one almost black.

That is the dog they all looked at as Joe Carraclough stood there, having told no lie, having only asked a question. They all stood, waiting the duke's verdict.

But the duke said nothing. He only walked forward, slowly, as if he were seeing a dream. He bent beside the collie, looking with eyes that were as knowing about dogs as any Yorkshireman alive. And those eyes did not waste themselves upon twisted ears, or blotched marking, or rough head. Instead they were looking at a paw that the duke lifted, looking at the underside of the paw, staring intently at five black pads, crossed and recrossed with the scars where thorns had lacerated, and stones had torn.

For a long time the duke stared, and when he got up he did not speak in Yorkshire accents any more. He spoke as a gentleman should, and he said: "Joe Carraclough. I never owned this dog. 'Pon my soul, she's never belonged to me. Never!"

Then he turned and went stumping down the path, thumping his cane and saying: "Bless my soul. Four hundred miles! Damme, wouldn't ha' believed it. Damme—five hundred miles!"

He was at the gate when his granddaughter whispered to him fiercely.

"Of course," he cried. "Mind your own business. Exactly what I came for. Talking about dogs made me forget. Carraclough! Carraclough! What're ye hiding for?"

"I'm still here, sir."

"Ah, there you are. You working?"

"Eigh, now. Working," Joe said. That's the best he could manage. . . .

Then Mrs. Carraclough came to his rescue, as a good housewife in Yorkshire will.

"Why, Joe's got three or four things that he's been considering," she said, with proper display of pride. "But he hasn't quite said yes or no to any of them yet."

"Then say no quick," the old man puffed. "Had to sack Hynes. Didn't know a dog from a drunken filly. Should ha' known all along no damn Londoner could handle dogs fit for Yorkshire taste. How much, Carraclough?"

"Well, now," Joe began.

"Seven pounds a week, and worth every penny," Mrs. Carraclough chipped in. "One o' them other offers may come up to eight," she lied, expertly. For there's always a certain amount of lying to be done in life, and when a woman's married to a man who has made a lifelong cult of being honest, then she's got to learn to do the lying for two.

"Five," roared the duke—who, after all, was a Yorkshireman, and couldn't help being a bit sharp about things that pertained to money.

"Six," said Mrs. Carraclough.

"Five pound ten," bargained the duke, cannily.

"Done," said Mrs. Carraclough, who would have been willing to settle for three pounds in the first place. "But, o' course, us gets the cottage too."

"All right," puffed the duke. "Five pounds ten and the cottage. Begin Monday. But—on one condition.

254

Carraclough, you can live on my land, but I won't have that thick-skulled, screw-lugged, gay-tailed eyesore of a misshapen mongrel on my property. Now never let me see her again. You'll get rid of her?"

He waited, and Joe fumbled for words. But it was the boy who answered, happily, gaily: "Oh, no, sir. She'll be waiting at school for me most o' the time. And, anyway, in a day or so we'll have her fixed up and coped up so's ye'd never, never recognize her."

"I don't doubt tht," puffed the duke, as he went to the car. "I don't doubt ye could do just exactly that …."

# Dog Sayings
## And what they mean

## You're barking up the wrong tree
*You're looking in the wrong place.*

## He who lies down with dogs, rises with fleas
*Some people have bad habits, just like dogs have fleas.*
*If you spend too much time with them, you'll get them, too.*

## You can't teach an old dog new tricks

## Let sleeping dogs lie
*It's best to just leave old disagreements alone.*

*When people are used to doing things a certain way, they don't like to change.*

# ANTS GO MARCHING

The ants go march-ing one by one, Hur-- rah, _____ Hur - rah, _____ The ants go march - ing one by one, Hur-- rah, _____ Hur - rah, _____ The ants go march - ing one by one, The

lit - tle one stops to suck his thumb and they

all go march - ing

down _____ to the ground _____ to get

out _____ of the rain, Boom! Boom! Boom!

2 … two by two … tie his shoe …
3 … three by three … climb a tree …
4 … four by four … shut the door …
5 … five by five … take a dive …
6 … six by six … pick up sticks …

7 … seven by seven … pray to heaven …
8 … eight by eight … shut the gate …
9 … nine by nine … check the time …
10 … ten by ten … say "THE END!"

# ANT FARM

large glass jar, soil, a piece of paper,
ants, sponge, water, aluminum foil,
food, plastic wrap, rubber band

**A**lmost nothing in nature is as fascinating as a busy ant colony hard at work. Related to the honeybee and the wasp, ants are very social critters that work together to support their community. There are several types of ants: the workers, the soldiers, the babies, and the queen herself, who is usually mother to all the ants in a colony. Each ant group has its own job and is responsible for performing certain tasks. In order to remain so organized, ants touch each other with their antennae to communicate. To observe all the interesting habits and interactions of the ant world with your very own eyes, try making this simple ant farm.

1. Go outside to your backyard or park and hunt for anthills. Look for the telltale march of working ants carrying food, and follow them home.

2. Very carefully, without hurting any ants, collect the loose dirt around the anthill and put it into the jar. This makes for good ant-tunneling soil.

3. Before adding the ants, spray some water into the jar to lightly moisten the soil.

4. Use a small piece of paper to sweep the ants into the jar. Ask an adult to supervise, and be very careful, because some ants like to nip!

5. Once you have gathered a few dozen ants, wet a small bit of sponge and place it inside. Although ants get most of their water from food, this is always a good precaution.

6. Make a small food dish out of aluminum foil. For meals, ants love insects and sweet foods. A small piece of bread dipped in sugar water, tiny bits of watermelon, cookie crumbs, and dead caterpillars all make for good ant food.

7. Ants usually can't climb up the side of a jar, but you can seal it with a piece of plastic wrap punched with air holes and secured with a rubber band, just in case.

8. Every so often spray a little water into the jar to keep the soil moist for tunneling. Replace the foil dish and freshly wet the sponge each time you add food to the jar.

# BUG FACTS

✳ Peew! A stick insect found in Florida sprays a chemical
so foul-smelling it can make you pass out.

✳ Measuring less than a millimeter in length, tiny mites
often hitch a ride on the bodies of larger insects.

✳ The honeybee has two stomachs—one to hold
the honey it's collected, and one to digest food.

✳ In its lifetime, a worker honeybee produces

✳ The Nephila spider of New Guinea is so large its
web is used as a fishing net by local fishermen.

✳ The glow worm, found in the caves of New Zealand, grows brighter as its
appetite increases to lure other insects to fly nearer for easy capture.

* An ant can lift up to 50 times its own body weight.

* Crickets have ears on their front legs!

* An inchworm isn't actually an inch long.
Its length can vary from 3 millimeters to 6 centimeters.

* A cockroach can survive for over a week without its head!

an average of 1/12 of a teaspoon of honey.

* The owl butterfly has a unique way to send
its enemies running. It simply opens up
its wings to reveal markings that
mimic the ominous eyes of an owl.

# BUG JUICE

**H**ere is a delicious and healthy version of a traditional camp favorite. And no, there aren't any bugs in bug juice!

1 cup pineapple juice

1 cup orange juice

½ cup lemon juice

1 cup red grape juice

1 cup cranberry juice

2 cups apple juice

2 cups cold water

Ice cubes

1 orange

1. Combine juices in a large pitcher, add ice and stir well.

2. Garnish with orange slices and serve chilled with a plate of your favorite animal crackers.

*Serves eight*

# THE BUTTERFLY MYTH

Long ago, after the Creator had shaped the world from mud, the north wind came to cool the air. The leaves started to change colors, and the sunlight didn't stay so long. This made the Creator very sad. "I have given a season to everything, and so everything must die away. The leaves will dry up, the flowers will fade, and even the beautiful children will grow up and grow old." Filled with sorrow, the Creator's heart was heavy.

As he watched the children playing, he tried to think of a way to ease his pain. He looked at the bright blueness of the sky; he marveled at the shiny blackness of a little girl's hair; and he found joy in the yellows and reds of the turning leaves. "Soon the sky will be gray," he said, "so too the young girl's hair. The leaves will dry to dust. I must find a way to preserve all these beautiful colors that make my heart glad."

The Creator gathered all the colors: a touch of the sun's golden rays, the black of the little girl's hair, a patch of blue sky, some purple and red petals from the late-blooming flowers, the blades of the bright green grasses, the white of the ground cornmeal, and on and on. He put these colors into his magical bag and added the songs of birds. He gave the bag to the children. "Children, this gift will make your hearts glad. Open it and you'll discover a wonderful surprise inside."

The children opened the bag, and hundreds of brilliantly colored butterflies flew out and sang as they darted about. The children had never seen anything so beautiful. They joyfully mimicked their songs and their dancing.

But soon the birds came and complained to the Creator. They were angry that the butterflies sang their songs. So they scolded the Creator: "It is not right that you've shared our songs. Each of our melodies is unique and should belong to us alone."

"You are right," agreed the Creator. "I should not have taken what is yours." So the Creator silenced the butterflies' voices.

And that is how the butterflies came to be.

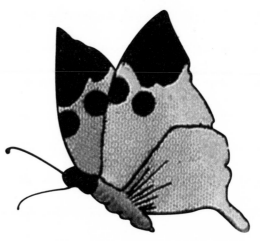

# HUMMINGBIRD AND BUTTERFLY GARDEN

They may not be related, but butterflies and hummingbirds share a passion for the nectar found in many flowers. Lucky for us, that means a garden designed to attract hummingbirds will draw butterflies as well! Whether it's a Monarch butterfly or a Calliope hummingbird—the tiniest bird in America—that visits your flowerbed, both species are remarkable creatures that will bring a dash of color to the yard.

- Keep all your nectar-rich flowers planted together to attract a crowd. The tallest plants should be placed near the house, where there is less wind (this helps hummers and butterflies to sup, and also gives you a better view of them as they hover about). Some hummingbirds can flap their wings at a rate of 200 times per second! Choose red flower varieties, which hummingbirds are most attracted to. Trumpet-shaped blossoms enable their long beaks to reach inside the flower.

- To attract butterflies, leave that milkweed alone the next time you're weeding. Butterflies love the wild plant, and you just might find a caterpillar or two feeding on them. There are well over 11,000 different kinds of butterflies and moths in North America alone. Like birds, many types of butterflies migrate during winter. With a good insect guide, you can trace their route south.

- Some suggested plants to attract both butterflies and hummingbirds: bleeding heart, butterfly bush, hollyhock, lupine, verbena, fuchsia, firecracker vine, exotic love vine, bee balm, columbine, honeysuckle, delphinium, iris, phlox, rhododendron, snapdragon. Butterflies are also particularly partial to sunflowers, sweet alyssum, annual cone flowers, common cosmos, black-eyed Susans, and zinnias.

# THE STORKS

On the outskirts of a small village, atop an old deserted house, lived a family of storks— a mother stork, a father stork, and their four baby storks. The father stork was a very serious bird who spent many hours standing on one of his long legs guarding his family. He was so quiet and still that from afar he looked like a statue made of stone. The baby storks often amused themselves by trying to trick or surprise their father into moving, but he never did. The mother stork was very loving and kind to her young children, despite their disobedient ways.

"We want to play!" they cried to their mother. "We want to play like the little human children do. Why must we learn to fly all day long?"

The mother stork, who was very patient, gently explained how all baby storks must learn to fly before the winter so they can fly to the Summer Country where it is warm and beautiful.

"In the Summer Country, you may play as much as you wish," she promised.

"But it's summer here," whined the little storks, "and we can see the children from our nest skipping and singing below and oh, it looks like so much fun."

## THE STORKS

"Now, now, dear ones," said the mother stork, "there is a time and a place for all things, and now is the time for learning. Your father is very disciplined in his task of guarding the nest, and so should you be in learning to fly." For the mother stork knew that in only a few short months all the storks of the land would be gathering to fly over the vast ocean to the Summer Country. She shuddered to think of the terrible fate that would befall her babies if they could not fly well enough to make the long journey.

One morning, when the young storks should have been practicing their take off positions, they snuck to the side of the roof to peek down at four boys passing by on their way to play leapfrog in the meadow.

"Ohhhh," moaned the littlest stork, "how I would love to leapfrog all the way to the pond and gobble down a tasty toad!" The other storks all agreed, and in their excitement made such a clamor that the four boys looked up to see what the racket was all about.

The oldest and meanest-looking boy started jeering at the baby storks, singing:

*"Storks, storks watch the time*
*When winter comes don't be*
*    left behind.*
*Baby storks that cannot fly*
*Mother and father must say good-bye.*
*For infant children they must bring*
*To human families in the spring.*
*While girls and boys grow smart and old*
*Baby storks die in winter's cold."*

Then the boys all laughed and walked on toward the meadow. The four little storks were terrified by what they'd

## THE STORKS

heard and ran to their father, who stood stiff and rigid beside their nest.

"Father, father," they cried, "is it true that we will be left behind and die of cold in winter?" The father stork did not answer. In fact, he did not even blink.

So the young storks ran to their mother, who was tidying up the nest, and asked her if the nasty song was true.

"Well," explained the mother stork, "it's true that adult storks deliver human babies to families that want them. There is a great pond in the Summer Country where all the babies sleep, floating on lily pads. It is our job to choose the right infant for each family and carry them back to this land. That is the way of things and we take our responsibilities very seriously."

"But mother," said the biggest of the young storks, "are storks that do not learn to fly left to die?"

"All storks would die," said the mother stork gently, "if they remained here past the fall. No stork can survive the long cold winter; it is just not in our nature. But never fear my little ones, your father and I will make sure you are all fine flyers by the time of the Gathering."

For the next few days the young storks tried extra hard to be disciplined in their studies, but were soon easily distracted. The boys now made it a habit of walking by their nest every day singing the ugly song as loudly as they could.

"Those boys are mean, mean, mean!" said the littlest stork. "Especially that older-looking one. He always sings the loudest."

"Yeah," the others agreed, and tried to think of ways to seek revenge on the boy.

All through the summer the young storks practiced their flying and the boys sneered their song as they passed by. Even when his friends grew tired of the song, the oldest boy would sing it alone twice as loud. Soon though, the young storks were flying on their own, and took to the sky to master the final and most difficult task of riding the wind.

The night before the Great Stork Gathering, the young storks settled on a plan to get back at the boy. They decided to follow him home that evening and drop frogs into his family's chimney.

From high above, the storks watched as the boy left his friends and entered a small cottage on the town square. They swooped down to get a better look and when they silently peeked through the window they saw a woman crying and rocking back and forth in an old rocking chair. The young boy, who no longer looked so mean, was trying to comfort her.

"Go away," the boy's mother sobbed, "I have lost my precious little baby to the Fever and I fear I will never have another. Now leave me, I wish to sit here alone and cry for my lost daughter." The storks watched as the boy, who looked so sad and lonely, slowly walked away, leaving his heartbroken mother alone in her misery. The storks crept from the window and quietly flew back to their nest to tell their mother what they had seen.

"Yes," said the mother stork calmly, "that child's parents were brought a new baby just this spring from the Summer Country. Sometimes children do not live to become young girls and boys. That is the way of things."

"But the boy looked upset, too," said the littlest stork. "He didn't seem very mean anymore. I felt bad for him."

"And well you should, for he has lost his baby sister and he is alone with his grieving parents. Sometimes," went on the mother stork, "humans feel so lonely and hurt inside that they take out their pain on the world around them. You should think twice about making that sad boy more unhappy."

The young storks thought long and hard about what their mother had told them and decided to eat up all the frogs they had collected, instead of dumping them down the boy's chimney.

The next day the Great Stork Gathering took place, and the young storks were finally ready to fly across the ocean to the Summer Country with their father and mother.

"By the time you return here next spring," said their mother as she covered up the nest for the winter, "you will no longer be children but full-grown storks

with human babies to deliver." The young storks had a hard time imagining they would ever be grown up, and doubted whether that spring day would actually come. But it was time for them to take their family's place in the Gathering and off they all went, gliding on the wind over the ocean, beginning their long flight.

Sure enough, winter came and went as it had in years before. Spring showed signs of its welcome arrival as the snow melted and the flowers began to bud. One crisp clear morning hundreds of storks appeared on the horizon, flying in from the Summer Country with little human babies held in their beaks. All the expectant families were waiting outside their homes, hoping that they would be lucky enough to receive a new little

# THE STORKS

girl or boy of their own. One by one the storks dropped their little bundles of joy into the grateful arms of the new mothers and fathers.

But there was one small family that was not waiting outside. The boy who jeered at the baby storks sat with his mother and father at the dinner table in silence as they listened to the happy voices of their neighbors in the square. When the boy could take it no more, he ran to his room and wept into his pillow so his parents wouldn't hear him. He had almost cried himself to sleep when he heard a quiet tapping on his window and saw four strong adult storks carrying a large sack between them. He opened the window and the four storks jumped inside. The storks gently laid a squirming bundle on the floor. The boy carefully unwrapped the parcel to find twin infant girls staring up at him! He let out a shout of joy and called to his mother and father. Within moments his parents each sat happily cuddling a baby. The boy looked up to thank the storks, but they were already gone. They had their own nests to build and families to raise. But before they went their separate ways, the once young storks flew down to the village pond and feasted on their favorite childhood meal of delicious green toads one last time.

277

# THE OWL AND THE PUSSY-CAT

The Owl and the Pussy-Cat went to sea
In a beautiful pea-green boat,
They took some honey,
 an plenty of money;
Wrapped up in a five-pound note.
The Owl looked up to the stars above,
And sang to a small guitar,
"O lovely Pussy, O Pussy, my love,
What a beautiful Pussy you are,
 You are,
 You are!
What a beautiful Pussy you are!"

Pussy said to the Owl, "You elegant fowl!
How charmingly sweet you sing!
O let us be married! too long we have tarried:
But what shall we do for a ring?"
They sailed away for a year and a day,
To the land where the Bong-tree grows,

And there in a wood a Piggy-wig stood,
With a ring at the end of his nose,
 His nose,
 His nose,
With a ring at the end of his nose.

"Dear Pig, are you willing to sell
 for one shilling
Your ring?" Said the Piggy, "I will."
So they took it away, and were married
 next day
By the Turkey who lives on the hill.
They dined on mince, and slices of quince,
Which they ate with a runcible spoon;
And hand in hand, on the edge of the sand,
They danced by the light of the moon,
 The moon,
 The moon,
They danced by the light of the moon.

# Cat Sayings

### And what they mean

## It's raining cats and dogs
*It's pouring!*

## Don't let the cat out of the bag
*Don't give away the secret....*

## Nervous as a cat in a room full of rocking chairs
*Sensing danger in every direction.*

## Cat's got your tongue
*You're speechless.*

When the cat's away

the mice will play

# STUART LITTLE

## BY E. B. WHITE

When Mrs. Frederick C. Little's second son arrived, everybody noticed that he was not much bigger than a mouse. The truth of the matter was, the baby looked very much like a mouse in every way. He was only about two inches high; and he had a mouse's sharp nose, a mouse's tail, a mouse's whiskers, and the pleasant, shy manner of a mouse. Before he was many days old he was not only looking like a mouse but acting like one, too—wearing a gray hat and carrying a small cane. Mr. and Mrs. Little named him Stuart, and Mr. Little made him a tiny bed out of four clothespins and a cigarette box.

One day when he was seven years old, Stuart was in the kitchen watching his mother make tapioca pudding. He was feeling hungry, and when Mrs. Little opened the door of the electric refrigerator to get something, Stuart slipped inside to see if he could find a piece of cheese. He supposed, of course, his mother had seen him, and when the door swung shut and he realized he was locked in, it surprised him greatly.

285

"Help!" he called. "It's dark in here. It's cold in this refrigerator. Help! Let me out! I'm getting colder by the minute."

But his voice was not strong enough to penetrate the thick wall. In the darkness he stumbled and fell into a saucer of prunes. The juice was cold. Stuart shivered, and his teeth chattered together. It wasn't until half an hour later that Mrs. Little again opened the door and found him standing on a butter plate, beating his arms together to try to keep warm, and blowing on his hands, and hopping up and down.

"Mercy!" she cried. "Stuart, my poor little boy."

"How about a nip of brandy?" said Stuart. "I'm chilled to the bone."

But his mother made him some hot broth instead, and put him to bed in his cigarette box with a doll's hot-water bottle against his feet. Even so, Stuart caught a bad cold, and this turned into bronchitis, and Stuart had to stay in bed for almost two weeks.

During his illness, the other members of the family were extremely kind to Stuart. Mrs. Little played tick-tack-toe with him. George made him a soap bubble pipe and a bow and arrow. Mr. Little made him a pair of ice skates out of two paper clips.

One cold afternoon Mrs. Little was shaking her dustcloth out of the window when she noticed a small bird lying on the windowsill, apparently dead. She brought it in and put it near the radiator, and in a short while it fluttered its wings and opened its eyes. It was a pretty little hen-bird, brown, with a streak of yellow on her breast. The Littles didn't agree on what kind of bird she was.

"She's a wall-eyed vireo," said George, scientifically.

"I think she's more like a young wren," said Mr. Little. Anyway, they fixed a place for her in the living room, and fed her, and gave her a cup of water. Soon she felt much better and went hopping around the house, examining everything with the greatest care and interest. Presently she hopped upstairs and into Stuart's room where he was lying in bed.

"Hello," said Stuart. "Who are you? Where did you come from?"

"My name is Margalo," said the bird, softly, in a musical voice. "I come from fields once tall with wheat, from pastures deep in fern and thistle; I come from vales of meadowsweet, and I love to whistle."

Stuart sat bolt upright in bed. "Say that again!" he said.

"I can't," replied Margalo. "I have a sore throat."

"So have I," said Stuart. "I've got bronchitis. You better not get too near me, you might catch it."

"I'll stay right here by the door," said Margalo.

"You can use some of my gargle if you want to," said Stuart. "And here are some nose drops, and I have plenty of Kleenex."

"Thank you very much, you are very kind," replied the bird.

"Did they take your temperature?" asked Stuart, who was beginning to be genuinely worried about his new friend's health.

"No," said Margalo, "but I don't think it will be necessary."

"Well, we better make sure," said Stuart, "because I would hate to have anything happen to you. Here...."

And he tossed her the thermometer. Margalo put it under her tongue, and she and Stuart sat very still for three minutes. Then she took it out and looked at it, turning it slowly and carefully.

"Normal," she announced. Stuart felt his heart leap for gladness. It seemed to him that he had never seen any creature so beautiful as this tiny bird, and he already loved her.

"I hope," he remarked, "that my parents have fixed you up with a decent place to sleep."

"Oh, yes," Margalo replied. "I'm going to sleep in the Boston fern on the bookshelf in the living room. It's a nice place, for a city location. And now, if you'll excuse me, I think I shall go to bed—I see it's getting dark outside. I always go to bed at sundown. Good night, sir!"

"Please don't call me 'sir,'" cried Stuart. "Call me Stuart."

"Very well," said the bird. "Good night, Stuart!" And she hopped off, with light, bounding steps.

"Good night, Margalo," called Stuart. "See you in the morning."

Stuart settled back under the bedclothes again. "There's a might fine bird," he whispered, and sighed a tender sigh.

When Mrs. Little came in, later, to tuck Stuart in for the night and hear his prayers, Stuart asked her if she thought the bird would be quite safe sleeping down in the living room.

"Quite safe, my dear," replied Mrs. Little.

"What about that cat Snowbell?" asked Stuart, sternly.

"Snowbell won't touch the bird," his mother said. "You go to sleep and forget all about it." Mrs. Little opened the window and turned out the light.

Stuart closed his eyes and lay there in the dark, but he couldn't seem to go to sleep. He tossed and turned, and the bedclothes got all rumpled up. He kept thinking about the bird downstairs asleep in the fern. He kept thinking about Snowbell and about the way Snowbell's eyes gleamed. Finally, unable to stand it any longer, he switched on the light. "There's just something in me that doesn't trust a cat," he muttered. "I can't sleep, knowing that Margalo is in danger."

Pushing the covers back, Stuart climbed out of bed. He put on his wrapper and slippers. Taking his bow and arrow and his flashlight, he tip-toed out into the hall. Everybody had gone to bed and the house was dark. Stuart found his way to the stairs and descended slowly and cautiously into the living room, making no noise. His throat hurt him, and he felt a little bit dizzy.

"Sick as I am," he said to himself, "this has got to be done."

Being careful not to make a sound, he stole across to the lamp by the book-shelf, shinnied up the cord, and climbed out onto the shelf. There was a faint ray of light from the street lamp outside, and Stuart could dimly see Margalo, asleep in the fern, her head tucked under her wing.

"Sleep dwell upon thine eyes, peace in thy breast," he whispered, repeating a speech he had heard in the movies. Then he hid behind a candlestick and waited, listening and watching. For half an hour he saw nothing, heard nothing but the faint ruffle of Margalo's wings when she stirred in dream. The clock struck ten, loudly, and before the sound of the last stroke had died away Stuart saw two gleaming yellow eyes peering out from behind the sofa.

"So!" thought Stuart. "I guess there's going to be something doing after all." He reached for his bow and arrow.

The eyes came nearer. Stuart was frightened, but he was a brave mouse, even when he had a sore throat. He placed the arrow against the cord of the bow and waited. Snowbell crept softly toward the bookshelf and climbed noiselessly up into the chair within easy reach of the Boston fern where Margalo was asleep. Then he crouched, ready to spring. His tail waved back and forth. His eyes gleamed bright. Stuart decided

the time had come. He stepped out from behind the candlestick, knelt down, bent his bow, and took careful aim at Snowbell's left ear—which was the nearest to him.

"This is the finest thing I have ever done," thought Stuart. And he shot the arrow straight into the cat's ear.

Snowbell squealed with pain and jumped down and ran off toward the kitchen.

"A direct hit!" said Stuart. "Thank heaven! Well, there's a good night's work done." And he threw a kiss toward Margalo's sleeping form.

It was a tired little mouse that crawled into bed a few minutes later— tired but ready for sleep at last.

# Animal Sayings

Quick as a bunny

Wise as an owl

Quiet as a mouse

Silly as a snake

Strong as an ox

Proud as a peacock

Cross as a bear

Stubborn as a mule

Mad as a wet hen

Busy as a bee

Blind as a bat

Gentle as a lamb

# THE NEWT

*by Natalie Joan*

"It's a newt! It's a newt!"
Cried the children all three.
Said the newt, "Why on earth
Are they fishing for me?

"I'm nothing to look at,
I'm no good to eat."
Cried Bet, "You're a beauty!"
Said Janie, "How sweet!"

"Much obliged, much obliged"
(With a sort of salute)
"But a beauty I'm not—
Never was," said the newt.

# SEA ANIMAL FACTS

✳ It takes 7 years for a lobster to grow to 1 pound.

✳ Next time you're floating down the Amazon, keep your eyes peeled for the rare pink dolphin. These beautiful but endangered sea mammals can also be found in Hong Kong.

✳ The eye of the giant squid

✳ Talk about a fish out of water! The climbing perch fish of India can survive for days on dry land. This unusual fish can use its fins and tail to walk along the ground in search of a new home when its old watering hole has dried up.

✳ A shark can grow a new set of teeth in just one week!

✳ Squids and octopuses have 3 hearts. Does that mean they're 3 times more loving than we are?

✳ Unlike humans, sharks have absolutely no bones. Their skeleton is made up entirely of cartilage.

✴ Starfish have one eye on the tip of each of their legs (usually five).

✴ The great blue whale is the world's largest mammal.
They are born weighing an average of 3 tons (that's 6,000 pounds!),
and an adult can weigh up to 150 tons.

can be up to a foot wide.

✴ Don't you wish you could suddenly turn into a giant
the next time someone bullies you at school? Well, the
puffer fish can do just that. When threatened, this prickly
little fish tries to scare off its enemies by swallowing enough water
to inflate itself up to several times its normal body mass.

✴ As for seahorses, it's the male, not the female, that carries and gives birth to
baby seahorses. The female seahorse lays its eggs in a pouch on the male
seahorse's belly, where he holds the eggs until they hatch.

✴ Never get into a staring contest with a shark. They don't blink!

# ANIMAL DIORAMAS

shoebox, construction paper, scissors, crayons,
markers, colored pencils, tape or glue, thread

*optional*: tissue paper, glitter, yarn,
pipe cleaners, cotton balls, pebbles

**I**s your neighborhood too small to have its own ocean? Do the houses next door block your African vistas? Does your basement lack the headroom for a full-grown elephant? No problem! All you need is a little creativity and that shoebox sitting in the back of your closet. From underwater seascapes, to dinosaurs romping with honeybees, there is no limit to the worlds you can craft with a good set of colored pencils, paper, and your imagination.

1. Turn the bottom of the shoebox on its side and trim a sheet of construction paper so that it will fit snugly in the back of the box.

2. Draw a background scene onto it, like a volcanic mountain or a vast underwater abyss, depending on your theme. For extra decoration try gluing on glitter for the stars, cotton balls for the clouds, or saran wrap to create the illusion of water.

3. Now it's time to add the animals! For an underwater diorama, make colored cutouts of various fish, whales, seahorses, or whatever else sparks your imagination. A sky scene might include flying birds and insects. If land animals are your thing, try making a jungle habitat filled with wild beasts, a prehistoric landscape dotted with dinos, or a farmyard packed with pigs, horses, and little chicks.

4. To make your animals appear to be swimming or flying, use glue or tape to attach them to a piece of thread. Paste the other end of the thread to the top of the inside of the box. Animals on the ground can be kept in place using a little glue.

5. Now add the finishing touches. Make plants from colored tissue paper, seaweed from pipe cleaners, boulders out of pebbles. Put in anything that strikes your fancy. You can even make a story using several shoeboxes featuring recurring animal characters and their adventures.

# OCEAN SOUP

This is an easy and healthy dish to serve, and if the kids think the spinach is actually seaweed, they may even eat it along with the shells and the fish!

6 cups chicken broth

8 ounces mini pasta shells

3—4 cups spinach,
sliced into strips
and well-rinsed

2 cups goldfish crackers

1. In a large stockpot, bring broth to a low boil. Add pasta and continue to simmer for the length of time indicated on the pasta box.

2. Add spinach to soup, stirring slowly for about 1 minute.

3. Toss a handful of goldfish crackers on top and serve immediately.

*Serves four*

# THE WALRUS AND THE CARPENTER

BY LEWIS CARROLL

The sun was shining on the sea,
    Shining with all his might:
He did his very best to make
    The billows smooth and bright—
And this was odd, because it was
    The middle of the night.

The moon was shining sulkily,
    Because she thought the sun
Had got no business to be there
    After the day was done—
"It's very rude of him," she said,
    "To come and spoil the fun!"

The sea was wet as wet could be,
    The sands were dry as dry.
You could not see a cloud, because
    No cloud was in the sky:
No birds were flying overhead—
    There were no birds to fly.

The Walrus and the Carpenter
    Were walking close at hand:
They wept like anything to see
    Such quantities of sand:
"If this were only cleared away,"
    They said, "it would be grand!"

"If seven maids with seven mops
    Swept it for half a year,
Do you suppose," the Walrus said,
    "That they could get it clear?"
"I doubt it," said the Carpenter,
    And shed a bitter tear.

"O Oysters, come and walk with us!"
    The Walrus did beseech.
"A pleasant walk, a pleasant talk,
    Along the briny beach:
We cannot do with more than four,
    To give a hand to each."

The eldest Oyster looked at him,
　　But never a word he said:
The eldest Oyster winked his eye,
　　And shook his heavy head—
Meaning to say he did not choose
　　To leave the oyster-bed.

But four young Oysters hurried up,
　　All eager for the treat:
Their coats were brushed,
　　their faces washed,
　　Their shoes were clean and neat—
And this was odd, because, you know,
　　They hadn't any feet.

Four other Oysters followed them,
　　And yet another four;
And thick and fast they came at last,
　　And more, and more, and more—
All hopping through the frothy waves,
　　And scrambling to the shore.

The Walrus and the Carpenter
　　Walked on a mile or so,
And then they rested on a rock
　　Conveniently low:
And all the little Oysters stood
　　And waited in a row.

"The time has come," the Walrus said,
　　"To talk of many things:
Of shoes—and ships—and
　　sealing wax—
　　Of cabbages—and—kings—
And why the sea is boiling hot—
　　And whether pigs have wings."

"But wait a bit," the Oysters cried,
　　"Before we have our chat;
For some of us are out of breath,
　　And all of us are fat!"
"No hurry!" said the Carpenter.
　　They thanked him much for that.

"A loaf of bread," the Walrus said,
    "Is what we chiefly need:
Pepper and vinegar besides
    Are very good indeed—
Now, if you're ready, Oysters dear,
    We can begin to feed."

"But not on us!" the Oysters cried,
    Turning a little blue.
"After such kindness, that would be
    A dismal thing to do!"
"The night is fine," the Walrus said.
    "Do you admire the view?

"It was so kind of you to come!
    And you are very nice!"
The Carpenter said nothing but
    "Cut us another slice.
I wish you were not quite so deaf—
    I've had to ask you twice!"

"It seems a shame," the Walrus said,
    "To play them such a trick.
After we've brought them out so far,
    And made them trot so quick!"
The Carpenter said nothing but
    "The butter's spread too thick!"

"I weep for you," the Walrus said:
    "I deeply sympathize."
With sobs and tears he sorted out
    Those of the largest size,
Holding his pocket-handkerchief
    Before his streaming eyes.

"O Oysters," said the Carpenter,
    "You've had a pleasant run!
Shall we be trotting home again?"
    But answer came there none—
And this was scarcely odd, because
    They'd eaten every one.

There's
more than
one fish in
the sea

# Animal Sayings
### And what they mean

## The world is my oyster
*Everything is going my way!*

## Crocodile tears
*Fake tears, used to trick someone into thinking you're sad.*

## Like a fish
## out of water
*Out of your comfort zone.*

## Snug as a bug in a rug
*All cuddled up and tucked in tight.*

## I smell a rat
*Something suspicious is going on here.*

## You can catch more flies with honey than with vinegar
*It's easier to get what you want by being nice than by being a bully.*

# SHOO FLY

Shoo, fly, don't both - er me, Shoo, fly, don't both - er me,

Shoo, fly, don't both - er me, For I be - long to some-bod - y.

I feel, I feel, I feel, I feel like a morn-ing star, I

feel, I feel, I feel, I feel like a morn-ing star.

# CRICKET THERMOMETER

cricket, wristwatch, pencil, paper, friend

The animal kingdom is full of small wonders that abound in your very own backyard! Listen closely the next time you hear the crickets calling at night. That distinctive chirp is the sound they make when they rub their wings together. But did you know that you can tell the temperature by how frequently a cricket chirps?

The metabolism of a cricket, like other coldblooded insects, increases and decreases with the air temperature. As it gets warmer outside, a cricket's metabolism speeds up and it chirps more often. Cooler temperatures slow down a cricket's metabolism, causing it to chirp less. So the next time you hear a cricket sing, try this formula to calculate the temperature.

1. On a late summer evening, listen for the sound of a cricket chirping.

2. Count the number of chirps you hear while a friend measures off 15 seconds on his or her watch. Write it down.

3. Add 40 to the resulting number, and you have the approximate temperature in degrees Fahrenheit.

# THE ELEPHANT & THE BUTTERFLY

### BY E. E. CUMMINGS

Once upon a time there was an elephant who did nothing all day.

He lived by himself in a little house away at the very top of a curling road.

From the elephant's house, this curling road went twisting away down and down until it found itself in a green valley where there was another little house, in which a butterfly lived.

One day the elephant was sitting in his little house and looking out of his window doing nothing (and feeling very happy because that was what he liked most to do) when along this curling road he saw somebody coming up and up toward his little house; and he opened his eyes wide, and felt very much surprised. "Whoever is that person who's coming up along and along the curling road toward my little house?" the elephant said to himself.

And pretty soon he saw that it was a butterfly who was fluttering along the curling road ever so happily; and the elephant said: "My goodness, I wonder if he's coming to call on me?" As the butterfly came nearer and nearer, the elephant felt more and more

# THE ELEPHANT & THE BUTTERFLY

excited inside of himself. Up the steps of the little house came the butterfly and he knocked very gently on the door with his wing. "Is anyone inside?" he asked.

The elephant was ever so pleased, but he waited.

Then the butterfly knocked again with his wing, a little louder but still very gently, and said: "Does anyone live here, please?"

Still the elephant never said anything because he was too happy to speak.

A third time the butterfly knocked, this time quite loudly, and asked: "Is anyone at home?" And this time the elephant said in a trembling voice: "I am." The butterfly peeped in at the door and said: "Who are you, that live in this little house?" And the elephant peeped out at him and answered: "I'm the elephant who does nothing all day." "Oh," said the butterfly, "and may I come in?" "Please do," the elephant said with a smile, because he was very happy. So the butterfly just pushed the little door open with his wing and came in.

Once upon a time there were seven trees which lived beside the curling road. And when the butterfly pushed the door with his wing and came into the elephant's little house, one of the trees said to one of the trees: "I think it's going to rain soon."

318

# THE ELEPHANT & THE BUTTERFLY

"The curling road will be all wet and will smell beautifully," said another tree to another tree.

Then a different tree said to a different tree: "How lucky for the butterfly that he's safely inside the elephant's little house, because he won't mind the rain."

But the littlest tree said: "I feel the rain already," and sure enough, while the butterfly and the elephant were talking in the elephant's little house away at the top of the curling road, the rain simply began falling gently everywhere; and the butterfly and the elephant looked out of the window together and they felt ever so safe and glad, while the curling road became all wet and began to smell beautifully just as the third tree had said.

Pretty soon it stopped raining and the elephant put his arm very gently around the little butterfly and said: "Do you love me a little?"

And the butterfly smiled and said: "No, I love you very much."

Then the elephant said: "I'm so happy, I think we ought to go for a walk together you and I: for now the rain has stopped and the curling road smells beautifully."

The butterfly said: "Yes, but where shall you and I go?"

319

# THE ELEPHANT & THE BUTTERFLY

"Let's go away down and down the curling road where I've never been," the elephant said to the little butterfly. And the butterfly smiled and said: "I'd love to go with you away and away down the curling road—let's go out the little door of your house and down the steps together—shall we?" So they came out together and the elephant's arm was very gently around the butterfly. Then the littlest tree said to his six friends: "I believe the butterfly loves the elephant as much as the elephant loves the butterfly, and that makes me very happy, for they'll love each other always."

Down and down the curling road walked the elephant and the butterfly.

The sun was shining beautifully after the rain.

The curling road smelled beautifully of flowers.

A bird began to sing in a bush, and all the clouds went away out of the sky and it was Spring everywhere.

When they came to the butterfly's house, which was down in the green valley which had never been so green, the elephant said: "Is this where you live?"

And the butterfly said: "Yes, this is where I live."

# THE ELEPHANT & THE BUTTERFLY

"May I come into your house?" said the elephant.

"Yes," said the butterfly. So the elephant just pushed the door gently with his trunk and they came into the butterfly's house. And then the elephant kissed the butterfly very gently and the butterfly said: "Why didn't you ever before come down into the valley where I live?" And the elephant answered, "Because I did nothing all day. But now that I know where you live, I'm coming down the curling road to see you every day, if I may— and may I come?" Then the butterfly kissed the elephant and said: "I love you, so please do."

And every day after this the elephant would come down the curling road which smelled so beautifully (past the seven trees and the bird singing in the bush) to visit his little friend the butterfly.

And they loved each other always.

# THE MULTILINGUAL MYNAH BIRD

*BY JACK PRELUTSKY*

He can talk to you in Japanese,
Italian, French and Portuguese;
and even Russian and Chinese
the mynah bird will learn with ease.

Birds are known to cheep and chirp
and sing and warble, peep and purp,
and some can only squeak and squawk,
but the mynah bird is able to talk.

The mynah bird, the mynah bird,
a major, not a minor bird;
you'll never find a finer bird
than the multilingual mynah bird.

The multilingual mynah bird
can say most any word he's heard,
and sometimes he invents a few
(a very difficult thing to do).

So if you want to buy a bird,
why don't you try the mynah bird?
You'll never find a finer bird
than the multilingual mynah bird.

# ANIMAL GROUP NAMES

Here are the correct names for different groups of animals.
Believe it or not, we didn't make these up!

| ANIMAL | GROUP NAME |
| --- | --- |
| Ants | a colony of ants |
| Bears | a sloth of bears |
| Buffalo | a gang of buffalo |
| Butterflies | a swarm of butterflies |
| Cats | a clowder of cats |
| Cattle | a drove of cattle |
| Chickens | a flock of chickens |
| Clams | a bed of clams |
| Crows | a murder of crows |
| Dolphins | a pod of dolphins |
| Doves | a dole of doves |
| Elephants | a herd of elephants |
| Fish | a school of fish |
| Flies | a cloud of flies |
| Foxes | a skulk of foxes |
| Frogs | an army of frogs |
| Giraffes | a tower of giraffes |
| Goats | a trip of goats |
| Geese | a gaggle of geese |
| Gorillas | a band of gorillas |

| ANIMAL | GROUP NAME |
|--------|-----------|
| Horses | a team of horses |
| Hummingbirds | a charm of hummingbirds |
| Jellyfish | a smack of jellyfish |
| Kangaroos | a troop of kangaroos |
| Leopards | a leap of leopards |
| Lions | a pride of lions |
| Mice | a nest of mice |
| Otters | a raft of otters |
| Owls | a parliament of owls |
| Ox | a yoke of ox |
| Penguins | a rookery of penguins |
| Pigs | a drove of pigs |
| Prairie Dogs | a town of prairie dogs |
| Quails | a bevy of quails |
| Rhinoceros | a crash of rhinoceros |
| Sharks | a shiver of sharks |
| Swans | a game of swans |
| Tigers | an ambush of tigers |
| Toads | a knot of toads |
| Turtles | a bale of turtles |
| Wallabies | a mob of wallabies |
| Weasels | a gang of weasels |
| Wolves | a pack of wolves |
| Zebras | a crossing of zebras |

# MODOC

*BY RALPH HELFER*

*Modoc is the true story of a deep friendship shared by an elephant and a boy. Bram—the son of a circus elephant trainer, and Modoc—the child of the circus' star elephant, are born on the same day within the same hour. Their bond is instantaneous. Together they face a life filled with adventures, dangers, heartaches, and joys. In this excerpt, Modoc and Bram are introduced for the first time by Katrina, Bram's mother.*

This was an important moment, a beginning, for she knew the boy would spend his life with animals, especially elephants, and the meeting was of utmost importance. Neither the elephant nor the baby said a word. All was quiet as they looked at each other. Mo's small trunk wormed its way up, reaching to the baby. As Bram leaned over, his little hand pulled loose from Katrina's grasp, found its way down toward the trunk. A finger extended to meet the tip of the trunk. Bram's expression was one of curiosity; he felt the wet tip, Modoc moved her "finger" all around Bram's hand, sliding it across each finger and the palm. A big tickle grin spread across Bram's face, Modoc did her elephant "chirp," a tear glistened as it ran down Katrina's face. All was well. The future had been written.

# MODOC

From then on, Bram regularly joined them in the forest, with his toddling little feet tripping and falling along with Modoc's. They were each learning control of their bodies and minds. How to get body and mind to work together at the same time, on the same problem, was a constant challenge.

In the middle of the forest was a glade unique among all others. Large in size, it sat in an area the canopy of the forest didn't cover. Here the sun shone brightly and warmed thousands of flower blossoms. They were called God's Blanket, and came in every color: vivid crimson, burnt orange, sky blue, milky white, dark purple, with additional hues found only in magic places.

Bram and Modoc loved the glade. Bram would stand in the middle of the field, arms outstretched, eyes closed, inhaling the wonderful fragrance. Modoc, in her own way, would mimic him, her ears out, eyes only partly shut so she could watch Bram, trunk in the air, sucking in the sweet smell. They romped through the field, hand in trunk, both stumbling, rolling, giggling, and squeaking in their own way. Mo would drop to her chest and, pushing with her hind feet, plow up a row of the field flowers, then toss the loose ones over her head, sending a shower of brilliant colors through the air.

The two babies loved to feed each other. Standing on a log, Bram would hold the jug of milk as Modoc slurped away. Modoc's job was much easier; she could hold the baby bottle by wrapping her trunk around it and lowering it to Bram. Sometimes she would hold it out of reach and take a quick suck on it herself, until he started to cry or yelled for his mother. Then Modoc would hurriedly push it into Bram's mouth, in fear of being found out. Occasionally, in her haste, she would stick it in his ear or nose, which caused a bit of upset.

As the years passed, the babies grew quickly, with Modoc maturing more rapidly than Bram. At five years of age, Bram was only four feet tall and weighed forty-five pounds. Modoc was five feet tall and weighed a thousand pounds. At ten, Bram was five feet tall and weighed seventy pounds, Mo was eight feet tall and weighed thirty-five hundred pounds, yet she was still as much a youngster as Bram.

Early mornings found Modoc rocking back and forth waiting for Bram to appear so they could have breakfast together before he left for school. The first thing Bram did upon his return was run to Mo, giving her hugs and kisses. Early on, Modoc developed a special way of showing Bram her affection. She would put her trunk over Bram's shoulder and, snaking it around his waist, hold him tight, all the while making rumbling noises. It looked quite protective.

Modoc possessed a mischievous sense of humor. Sometimes while playing she would pick Bram up and walk off with him.... All Bram's yelling wouldn't get her to release him. She usually found a soft spot to drop him, like a nearby grass field. After, she would cock her head, lock her ears forward, lower the tip of her trunk to the ground, and emit a low guttural sound that was her way of saying, "Just kidding." Once, in an outrageously silly mood, she dumped him in a small stream, then ran as fast as she could, kicking up her heels and trumpeting all the way back to the barn.

Josef awoke one night to hear a loud cracking and breaking noise. He ran downstairs to find Modoc racing back and forth at the front door, trumpeting, and carrying on as though possessed. She had snapped her leg chain and crashed through one of the barn doors. He had never seen her act this way before. Why? Why at the front door to the house? His mind was racing. Bram! Josef flew upstairs to Bram's bedroom. Bram was laying stretched out diagonally on the bed, delirious, bathed in a pool of sweat.

Gathering the boy up, Josef raced downstairs, yelling for Katrina to get the truck key and a blanket. Curpo had arrived and was running toward the truck as fast as his small legs could take him. The tip of Mo's trunk traveled up and down Bram's prostrate body as she ran alongside Josef. Curpo had the truck door open as Josef laid Bram in Katrina's lap, and she bundled blankets around him. Mo stuck her trunk through the open window trying to touch Bram, rumbling all the while.

"He'll be okay, Mo. Now you just get back to the barn."

Josef, trying to believe his own words, jumped into the driver's seat and started the truck. It sped out of the driveway with Mo trumpeting and squealing, running after it. Curpo was waiting for Mo as she dragged herself up the driveway, exhausted and depressed. Mo didn't understand what was happening; she sensed that something was wrong and that her best friend was gone. Head low, her body trembling, she followed Curpo back to the barn.

Bram remained in the hospital for two weeks recovering from his illness. A deadly virus had chosen him for its victim, and had it not been for his quick arrival at the hospital, he might not have recovered at all. Josef didn't bother to tell the doctor about the strange occurrence of the psychic elephant alerting the family to Bram's illness.

The day Bram left the hospital, Josef stopped at a local farm to let him pick out Mo's choice of fruits and vegetables. Arriving home, Josef let Bram off at the barn, knowing he'd want to be alone with Modoc. Bram quietly opened the barn door and, walking on his toes, sneaked in, hoping to surprise her. As his eyes became accustomed to the half-darkness, he saw her standing with Emma. They were munching on a bale of hay.

"Mosie!" he yelled.

Modoc stopped mid-crunch. Throwing her ears forward, she blasted a trumpet that echoed throughout the barn. Bram ran to her, spilling half the food. She caught him with her trunk and held him in her special way. From her chest came her rumble of contentment. Bram wrapped his arms around her trunk and laid his head back against her chest. He knew that she had saved his life, and he loved her deeply for it.

"Whoever said you can't buy happiness forgot about puppies."—Gene Hill

# BINGO

There was a farm-er had a dog and Bin-go was his name - o.

B - I - N - G - O,   B - I - N - G - O,

B - I - N - G - O,   and   Bin-go was his   name - o.

2. There was a farmer had a dog and Bingo was his name-o.
 (Clap)-I-N-G-O, (Clap)-I-N-G-O, (Clap)-I-N-G-O,
And Bingo was his name-o.

There was a farmer had a dog and Bingo was his name-o.
(Clap)-(Clap)-N-G-O, (Clap)-(Clap)-N-G-O, (Clap)-(Clap)-N-G-O,
And Bingo was his name-o.

There was a farmer had a dog and Bingo was his name-o.
(Clap)-(Clap)-(Clap)-G-O, (Clap)-(Clap)-(Clap)-G-O, (Clap)-(Clap)-(Clap)-G-O,
And Bingo was his name-o.

There was a farmer had a dog and Bingo was his name-o.
(Clap)-(Clap)-(Clap)-(Clap)-O, (Clap)-(Clap)-(Clap)-(Clap)-O,
(Clap)-(Clap)-(Clap)-(Clap)-O,
And Bingo was his name-o.

There was a farmer had a dog and Bingo was his name-o.
(Clap)-(Clap)-(Clap)-(Clap)-(Clap), (Clap)-(Clap)-(Clap)-(Clap)-(Clap),
(Clap)-(Clap)-(Clap)-(Clap)-(Clap),
And Bingo was his name-o.

# BUT MOM DIDN'T LIKE DOGS

## BY DR. DONALD R. STOLTZ

We first met Chester, March second, 1965,
A shaggy, dirty bag of fur with big brown sorry eyes,
It was my sister's birthday, the day that she was eight,
When we saw him sitting in our yard, next to the garden gate.
We hurried out to pet him as fast as we could race,
And he almost had a smile on his straggly, lonely face.
But Mom didn't like dogs and said he couldn't stay,
And 'cause Mom didn't like dogs, she sent him on his way.

On April tenth of '65 we saw our friend again,
He was standing in the pouring rain outside the family den.
It was my father's birthday, and the house was full of guests;
So they really didn't miss us when we vanished from the rest.
We took a dish of ice cream and a piece of apple pie,
And when Father found us feeding Chet, a twinkle lit his eye.
But Mom didn't like dogs and said she was afraid,
And 'cause Mom didn't like dogs, she sent him on his way.

On June fifth of '65 it was birthday time again,
And Mom was having a party for the family and her friends.
When suddenly a commotion filled the summer air,
And there was Chester looking like a thrown-out teddy bear.
He looked so strange and funny, he made everybody laugh,
And Dad decided that our friend deserved a nice warm bath.
But Mom didn't like dogs—especially a stray,
And 'cause Mom didn't like dogs, she sent him on his way.

But by now we all were wondering and were really quite amazed
That Chester only seemed to come on very special days.
And when my birthday came around, the twelfth of that December,
I waited, watched, and wondered if Chester would remember.
By afternoon the heavy snows had piled up a drift
When through the storm I heard a bark, my special birthday gift.

But Mom didn't like dogs, so I pleaded and I prayed;
And though Mom didn't like dogs, she weakened, and he stayed.

Now many years have come and gone since 1965,
When we first met our dog, Chester, with the big brown sorry eyes.
And yesterday Pete, our postman, came and rang the back doorbell,
And told us he was retiring and had a tale to tell.
He told us he owned Chester, but back in '65,
He had to find a home for him after his wife died.
So each time we had a birthday and he delivered us a card,
He also would deliver Chester to our yard.
'Cause he knew how much we all loved dogs, and he knew that
     Mom would bend;
And although our mom never did like dogs,
     now Chester's her best friend.

# DOG FACTS

* To figure out how old your dog is in human years, count their first year as 15, their second year as 10, and each year after that as 5. For example, a 10-year-old dog would be about 65 in human years.

* The basenji from Africa is the only breed of dog that does not bark.

## A dog's sense of smell is up to one

* At 5 inches tall, the Chihuahua is the smallest breed of dog.

* The Australian dingo mates for life. When their partners die, dingoes have been known to mourn themselves to death.

* A seeing-eye dog cannot tell the difference between a red and green traffic light. Instead, it observes the moving cars to determine when it is safe to lead its owner across the street.

342

＊ The chow chow, a Chinese breed of dog, has a dark blue-black tongue. (And it didn't get that way from eating grape popsicles!)

＊ The Akita, a Japanese breed, has webbed feet, making it a top-notch swimmer.

# hundred times better than a person's.

＊ The first living creature to orbit the earth was a Russian dog named Laika (meaning "barker") on November 3, 1957.

＊ All domestic dogs descend from wolves.

＊ There are over 100 million dogs kept as pets worldwide.

# PAINTED ANIMAL COOKIES

**T**ransform simple sugar cookies into objects of animal art with this fun recipe. These scrumptious treats are sure to both satisfy your children's sweet tooth and inspire their creativity.

## COOKIE DOUGH:

*six tablespoons butter, room temperature*

*⅓ cup sugar*

*1 egg*

*⅔ cup honey*

*1 teaspoon vanilla*

*2¾ cups white flour, sifted*

*1 teaspoon baking soda*

*1 teaspoon salt*

*Animal cookie cutters*

## COOKIE PAINT:

*2 egg yolks*

*½ teaspoon water*

*Assorted food colorings*

*Small glazing brush*

1. Pre-heat oven to 375° F.

2. In a large bowl, combine butter, sugar, egg, honey, and vanilla. Mix well.

3. In another bowl, combine dry ingredients. Gradually add to butter mixture and mix well.

4. Wrap dough in waxed paper and refrigerate for at least 1 hour.

5. Roll dough out on floured surface to about ¼-inch thickness. Press cookie cutters into dough to make lots of different animal shapes. Transfer to a baking sheet, placing cookies about 2 inches apart.

6. Combine egg yolks and water in a small bowl and mix well to make cookie paint. Divide mixture among four small cups and add a drop of different food coloring to each cup to make a variety of bright colors.

7. Use glazing brush to paint your animals any way you want. Decorate with sprinkles as well, if desired.

8. Bake 8-10 minutes. For best colors, do not allow cookies to brown.

*Makes 5 dozen 2½-inch cookies*

# Animal Jokes

Why is it hard to talk
with a goat around?
*He keeps butting in.*

Why is an elephant an
unwelcome guest?
*Because he always brings his trunk.*

Why do ducks and geese
fly north in springtime?
*Because it is too far to walk.*

Why did the dalmatian
go to the eye doctor?
*Because he kept seeing spots.*

What do you get if you cross
a skunk and a teddy bear?
*Winnie the Phew.*

What kind of medicine
does a pig use?
*Oinkment.*

What do you call a
scared tyrannosaurus?
*A nervous Rex.*

What do you say to a cow if
she wakes up in bed with you?
*Mooooove over!*

What do you call a bee
who hums very quietly?
*A mumblebee.*

What is more amazing
than a talking dog?
*A spelling bee.*

# BEAR IN THERE

BY SHEL SILVERSTEIN

There's a Polar Bear
In our Frigidaire—
He likes it 'cause it's cold in there.
With his seat in the meat
And his face in the fish
And his big hairy paws
In the buttery dish,
He's nibbling the noodles,
He's munching the rice,
He's slurping the soda,
He's licking the ice.
And he lets out a roar
If you open the door.
And it gives me a scare
To know he's in there—
That Polary Bear
In our Fridgitydaire.

Mosquito
at my ear—
does it think
I'm deaf?

—Kobayashi Issa

# ACKNOWLEDGMENTS

"The Elephant and the Butterfly", from FAIRY TALES by E.E. Cummings. Copyright © 1965, 1993 by the Trustees for the E.E. Cummings Trust. Used by permission of Liveright Publishing Corporation.

"Mosquito at my ear" by Kobayashi Issa from THE ESSENTIAL HAIKU: VERSIONS OF BASHO, BUSON & ISSA, edited and with an introduction and selection copyright © 1994 by Robert Hass. Introduction and selection copyright © 1994 by Robert Hass. Unless otherwise noted, all translations copyright © 1994 by Robert Hass. Reprinted by permission of HarperCollins Publishers Inc.

"Lassie Come Home" by Eric Knight. First published as a short story in the *Saturday Evening Post*. Copyright © 1938 by the Curtis Publishing Company. Copyright renewed 1966 by Jere Knight, Betty Noyes Knight, Winifred Knight Mewborn, and Jennie Knight Moore. Reprinted by permission of the Knight Management Trust.

"The Inch Worm" from the Motion Picture HANS CHRISTIAN ANDERSEN by Frank Loesser © 1951, 1952 (Renewed) FRANK MUSIC CORP. All Rights Reserved

"He was a Good Lion" from WEST WITH THE NIGHT by Beryl Markham. Copyright © 1942, 1983 by Beryl Markham. Reprinted by permission of North Point Press, a division of Farrar, Straus & Giroux, LLC.

"The Three Foxes" by A.A. Milne Illustrations by E.H. Shepard, from WHEN WE WERE VERY YOUNG by A.A. Milne, illustrations by E.H. Shepard, copyright 1924 by E.P. Dutton, renewed 1952 by A.A. Milne. Used by permission of Dutton Children's Books, an imprint of Penguin Putnam Books for Young Readers, a division of Penguin Putnam Inc.

Reprinted with permission of Simon & Schuster from SCARLETT SAVES HER FAMILY by Jane Martin and J.C. Suarès. Copyright © 1997 by The North Shore Animal League.

"The Dog" and "The Panther" Copyright © 1962, 1940 by Ogden Nash, renewed. Reprinted by permission of Curtis Brown, Ltd.

Excerpt of text of Koko's Kitten by Dr. Francine Patterson, © 1985 by The Gorilla Foundation (www.koko.org).

Illustrations from THE ARK OF FATHER NOAH AND MOTHER NOAH and NURSERY FRIENDS FROM FRANCE by Maud and Miska Petersham. Reprinted by permission of Marjorie Petersham.

THE TALE OF PETER RABBIT by Beatrix Potter. Copyright © Frederick Warne & Co., 1902, 1987. Reproduced with kind permission of Frederick Warne & Co.

"The Multilingual Mynah Bird" from ZOO DOINGS by Jack Prelutsky.

Text copyright © 1983 by Jack Prelutsky. Illustrations copyright © 1983 by Paul Zelinsky.

Pages 16-19 from MODOC by Helfer Ralph. Copyright © 1997 by Ralph Helfer. Reprinted by permission of HarperCollins Publishers Inc.

"Eletelephony" from TIRRA LIRRA by Laura Richards. Copyright © 1930, 1932 by Laura E. Richards; Copyright © renewed 1960 by Hamilton Richards. By permission of Little, Brown and Company (Inc.).

Text from "XXI" in THE LITTLE PRINCE by Antoine de Saint-Exupery, copyright 1943 and renewed 1971 by Harcourt, Inc. reprinted by permission of the publisher.

"BEAR IN THERE" by Shel Silverstein. Copyright © 1981 by Evil Eye Music, Inc.

THE UNICORN Words and Music by Shel Silverstein. TRO-© Copyright 1962 (Renewed) 1968 (Renewed) Hollis Music, Inc., New York, NY

"BUT MOM DIDN'T LIKE DOGS" Reprinted by permission of Dr. Donald R. Stoltz.

CHARLOTTE'S WEB Copyright 1952 by E.B. White Renewed © 1980 by E.B. White

STUART LITTLE Copyright 1945 by E.B. White Text copyright renewed © 1973 by E.B. White

From *The Velveteen Rabbit*, © 1922 The Estate of Margery Williams, published by Egmont Books Limited, London and used with permission.

## ILLUSTRATIONS

pg.1, 310: D. O'Rourke; pg. 8: Simpson; page 10 & 13: Beatrix Potter; pg. 18, 129: Lawrence Chesler; pg. 19: Francis Brundage; pg. 23: E. Dorothy Rees; pg. 28 & 29, 303: L. Leslie Brooke; pg. 31: J.M. Rock; pg. 39, 292: Honor C. Appleton; pg. 48: Kate Greenaway; pg. 49, 50: Caroline Hall; pg. 59, 176: Margaret Evans Price, pg. 73: Paul Thomas; pg. 80-81, 103: Will F Stecher; pg. 105: J.H.N. Cralgen; pg. 107: J.H.J. Fricero; pg. 112, 138, 172, 311, Case: Maud & Miska Petersham; pg. 130-131, 132-133, 184-185, 214-216: Megan Halsey; pg. 148: K.J. Fricero; pg. 150-151: Florence Harrison; pg. 171: Jessie Wilcox Smith; pg. 288: Helena Macguire; pg. 179, 221: Blanche Fisher Wright, pg.183, 205: Frederick Richardson; pg.186: Lynne Bogue Hunt; pg. 199: M.A. Peart; pg 217: Harrison Cody; pg. 233: A.W.; pg. 249: Hy Hintermeister; pg. 268: Anne Anderson; pg. 272-273: Hansi; pg. 296: M.D. Johnston; pg. 314 & 316: Helen Munsell Roberts; pg. 326: Louis Wain; pg. 329: Hilda Austin; pg. 336: Charles Robinson; pg. 348: Shel Silverstein;